W9-AFS-759

"I don't know why you went through with the wedding!"

"Why else?" John removed his hands from his pockets, taking one step toward her. "Your father and I both got what we wanted out of this arrangement. He got the money he needed and I got what money usually can't buy. I'm an insider now. I belong! Proper Boston is never going to close its doors to me again."

"Is that so important?" Serena raged. "Does it really matter to you?"

"What do you think?" he asked unpleasantly, taking another step toward her, forcing her to retreat. "Why else would I marry you?"

Why else indeed? she asked herself, defeated. She should have known that from the start. There was no love here and never had been—except what she felt for him. *Had* felt, she corrected quickly. What she'd felt last summer....

Elizabeth Barnes lives with her husband and son near Boston, Massachusetts. She likes to see treasures from the past lovingly restored and was instrumental in helping restore the local nineteenth-century church after it was badly damaged by fire. Vintage cars are a long-standing passion of the whole family.

Books by Elizabeth Barnes

HARLEQUIN ROMANCE
3056—NOW AND FOREVER
3158—A VINTAGE AFFAIR

HARLEQUIN PRESENTS
1328—IN SPITE OF THEMSELVES

Don't miss any of our special offers. Write to us at the following address for information on our newest releases.

Harlequin Reader Service
P.O. Box 1397, Buffalo, NY 14240
Canadian address: P.O. Box 603,
Fort Erie, Ont. L2A 5X3

LAST SUMMER'S
GIRL
Elizabeth Barnes

Harlequin Books

TORONTO • NEW YORK • LONDON
AMSTERDAM • PARIS • SYDNEY • HAMBURG
STOCKHOLM • ATHENS • TOKYO • MILAN
MADRID • WARSAW • BUDAPEST • AUCKLAND

If you purchased this book without a cover you should be aware that this book is stolen property. It was reported as "unsold and destroyed" to the publisher, and neither the author nor the publisher has received any payment for this "stripped book."

Original hardcover edition published in 1991
by Mills & Boon Limited

ISBN 0-373-03278-1

Harlequin Romance first edition August 1993

LAST SUMMER'S GIRL

Copyright © 1991 by Elizabeth Barnes.
All rights reserved. Except for use in any review, the reproduction or utilization of this work in whole or in part in any form by any electronic, mechanical or other means, now known or hereafter invented, including xerography, photocopying and recording, or in any information storage or retrieval system, is forbidden without the permission of the publisher, Harlequin Enterprises Limited, 225 Duncan Mill Road, Don Mills, Ontario, Canada M3B 3K9.

All the characters in this book have no existence outside the imagination of the author and have no relation whatsoever to anyone bearing the same name or names. They are not even distantly inspired by any individual known or unknown to the author, and all incidents are pure invention.

® are Trademarks registered in the United States Patent and Trademark Office and in other countries.

Printed in U.S.A.

CHAPTER ONE

"WHAT a mess!" The cabdriver threw up his hands as he slammed on his brakes. His cab was trapped again, held captive on one of Boston's narrow, twisting streets. The evening rush hour, never easy, had run amok: gridlock, fueled by the bone-chilling cold and unforgiving rain of an October night.

"Worse than ever," the driver muttered darkly, adding a string of pithily explicit expletives before turning in his seat to address his passenger. "We're going nowhere in a hurry, lady."

"That's all right," she assured him. "It's certainly not your fault. I should have taken a later flight, missed all this..."

"If you say so." Briefly, he checked the traffic, saw that he couldn't move, and then looked back at her again. Not bad, he thought: young and easygoing on a night when most of his rides had been middle-aged and fit to spit... "You from here, or just visiting?" he asked, prepared to break the tedium with a little conversation.

"From here," Serena told him, "all my life."

"A real Bostonian..." Old Yankee stock, he guessed— not that it took any great detective work; it stood to reason. She looked the part—slender, attractive in a way that wasn't showy, and the curves hidden beneath her crumpled raincoat were likely to be nice but not spectacular. Her clothes were a little dull by his standards, although they looked to be good quality. Maybe that was the "understated elegance" he kept hearing about, the look classy people were said to have. Definitely, he decided, she came from high-class old money; her appearance gave it away. So did her address—the right side of Beacon Hill; you didn't have to be old Yankee stock to live there, but it helped. "You're a real blue blood, I bet."

"Whatever that means." She stiffened slightly, staring with unseeing eyes into the city night, where the rain-slicked pavement caught and reflected random patterns of light. "I've never thought it meant a thing."

"Well, no," he allowed approvingly—nice that she wasn't stuck-up about it, "but people look at Beacon Hill, see those cobblestones and gas lamps, and like to think that the old families are still around..." The traffic suddenly eased, enough to permit him to gain most of a block. "You live there with your parents?"

"No. My husband."

The cabbie whistled. "Gee—you kids! You start out with everything! What's left to look forward to when you start out with a home on Beacon Hill?"

"It's not very big." No, not very big, she thought, but it was a gem—a fine restoration, tastefully decorated, plenty of good antiques—but it was an empty shell, not a home. Appearance was all that mattered . . . "It's only got six rooms."

"Still—Beacon Hill . . ." He inched the cab forward, making it through one intersection before traffic stalled again. "Already married, a house on Beacon Hill . . . you and your husband—you've got it all."

All? What a joke that was! she told herself, withdrawing into her thoughts. All she and John had were possessions. Theirs was no real marriage; it was a pretense, a cold, bloodless arrangement that they accepted because neither of them really cared . . .

"Funny," he'd said, not in the least put out when she'd announced that she wouldn't sleep with him. "I expected you to say that." And later that evening, when she'd been transferring her things from his bedroom to the little guest room, he'd made clear what did bother him about her decision. "I see you're settling in," he'd observed, pausing in the open doorway to survey the confusion, "but I should warn you...I've never let anyone cheat me before, and I'm not about to start now."

"Don't worry," she'd told him, forcing herself to meet and hold his dark gaze. "I'll entertain for you, go to the right parties...whatever you want me to do for you socially. Just don't expect anything of me when we're alone."

"I know. You've made that very clear." He'd smiled— a strange, unreadable smile, stretching the silence almost to breaking point before he'd finally moved away, leaving her alone in the chaste little room.

"Now we'll make some progress," the cabbie announced as he turned on to a side street, leaving the worst of the congestion behind. "See? There's the State House." He gestured as it came into view, the pristine golden dome glittering in the rainy night. "Funny thing," he mused, "I'm old enough to remember when it was the tallest thing on the hill. Now they've built all those buildings behind it—and it's still in charge. Know what I mean?"

"Yes." She did. The mellow brick and gold dome still dominated Beacon Hill; the Bullfinch design had not been diminished by the towering new constructions... some of them, for all she knew, built by John.

"Almost there," the cabdriver said, turning on to a side street, then once more into the small cobblestone lane. "You said number five?"

"Yes."

It stood at the end of the court, a spare and solid design: three storys of old brick, uncompromising granite lintels over the black door and each window, black shutters and black window boxes. There were, she saw, more lights on than usual, giving the illusion of welcome and warmth.

"Looks like you're expected," the cabdriver said as the front door opened. "That your husband?"

"Yes." Her breath caught as she watched the long and lithe figure come down the steps. She had forgotten, she realized as he stopped at the edge of the narrow pavement, ignoring the rain as he waited for the cab to pull up beside him—three days and nights away from him had blurred her memory—she had forgotten just how impressive—and attractive—her husband was. Illuminated by the street lamp, he was a tall, lean figure, his formal business suit unable to completely obscure his hard-muscled strength. He had a face like a dark angel's, clean and deeply incised: a long, finely chiseled nose, firm and thrusting jaw, a mouth which could appear ruthless, even cruel, until he smiled. Which he was doing now, Serena saw, absorbing that knowing expression of private amusement, the sensual curve of his lips.

"I'll take care of the cab," he told her as she fumbled with her purse. He leaned in to help her out, his hands at her waist when she was beside him on the pavement. "I'm surprised." He smiled, reading the confusion in her face. "You're home early."

"My mistake." She stared stonily back at him, trying to work out this sudden change. It had been nearly a month—the night she'd moved her things out of his room—since he'd touched her, nearly a month since he'd spoken to her with anything more than remote politeness in his tone. Why a change now? she wondered, more concerned by this new turn of events than she cared to admit. "I didn't see any point in hanging around after the conference ended, so I took the next flight back here." She paused briefly, just long enough to give special emphasis to what she said next. "I wish I'd waited for the last one of the day."

"Of course," he agreed, an ironic edge to his voice, "to miss the traffic."

"Among other things," she replied with an edge of her own.

"Yes." His edge, she noted, was getting harder. "I wonder why you didn't think to stay on for a few extra days. You could have had yourself a little holiday."

"What? And disappoint..." she extended the moment, watching the way he was watching her, seeing the sharp, questioning spark in his eyes "... Professor Brandenson?"

"No, we couldn't have that." His hands had remained at her waist; now she felt their pressure increase just enough to draw her closer. "Well, no matter why, you're home now. I missed you."

"That's——" Absurd, she'd intended to say, but he'd cut the word off at the source by the simple expedient of kissing her, and very thoroughly too. What was going on? she asked herself, caught by surprise, forced to reach for his shoulder to steady herself. This was making no sense, unless... Had he been rethinking their arrangement, deciding that he wanted more than this bizarre half a loaf? And if he did—that didn't bear thinking about! She shivered at the very idea, and instantly he released her.

"Poor girl, I'm keeping you here in the rain. But I'd better warn you—we have a guest. Cynthia's inside."

"What's she doing here?"

"It's a long story. She'll fill you in."

Glad to escape, Serena hurried inside to find her stepsister standing in the living-room doorway. Predictably, Cynthia was a picture of casual elegance: chocolate brown wool pants and an absolute dream of a pale pink silk blouse—the top three buttons left undone, the better to call attention to her more obvious charms, Serena noted uncharitably. Cynthia had surprisingly voluptuous curves for one so petite and delicate; she also had glorious spun-gold hair, light blue eyes and a glowing complexion. In a word, she was gorgeous—a reality Serena had accepted without bitterness when they'd been growing up together.

But she wasn't accepting it very well now, she discovered. No one had ever made the mistake of thinking Serena was gorgeous. She supposed that her features were pleasing enough, but there was nothing memorable about the oval of her face, the plain straight nose, the average mouth, whose tendency to curve into a too generous smile she usually managed to curb. Her eyes were medium brown; they matched the medium brown of her hair, which she usually wore pinned into a sensible and sedate twist at the back of her head.

It didn't bother her that she couldn't compete with Cynthia, but Serena was unhappily aware that tonight the contrast between them was more pronounced than usual. Although two years younger, Cynthia certainly had the edge in poise and maturity; in the face of her perfection, Serena's twist had begun to slip, the occasional errant curls escaping from the pins. Worse than that, she felt damp and crumpled. It had been a long day, and her simple beige wool suit was badly creased. She was an utter mess, she thought despairingly, then asked herself why she cared. There was no contest between her and Cynthia; it wasn't as though John was going to choose between them! Of course, if he ever did...well, any man would choose Cynthia, but what did that matter? It might be even better——

"Did John tell you why I'm here?" Cynthia demanded, interrupting a train of thought Serena was just as happy to abandon. "I've left Gregory, and Mummy and Dad are furious with me. They ordered me back to Houston—Houston, for heaven's sake!—but I'm not going. I can't!" She blinked, fighting tears. "Oh, Serena," Cynthia—who had never before in her life cried on Serena's shoulder—wailed, "it's just too awful!"

"Let it wait. Serena's had a long day," John advised, coming in out of the rain with the luggage, stopping

Cynthia dead in her tracks before addressing Serena. "You'll want to change, won't you?"

"I—yes, I suppose so," she agreed meekly, recognizing his question as no question at all.

"I'll bring your suitcase——" he gripped her arm, compelling her toward the staircase "—in case you want anything in it. It's no bother," he assured her when he saw her objection forming, his tone indulgent and slightly amused. "Didn't it occur to you that I might like a few minutes alone with my wife?"

No! she was tempted to say, but knew better—particularly when his fingers dug painfully into her flesh, warning her to keep quiet.

At the first landing, when she attempted to stop, John shook his head. "I had Mrs. Hutchins put Cynthia in the guest room of course," he said easily, but there was nothing easy about the way his dark gaze—smoldering and intent—held hers, nothing easy about the way he used his grip on her arm to force her up the second flight of stairs.

Toward his bedroom, Serena thought with a sinking feeling, toward the bedroom she'd vowed never again to enter, but it was obvious that she would have no say in the matter. Which was just like him, she fumed, an example of that incredible presence of his, the authority and sheer force of will he could exert whenever he wanted to get his own way.

But exactly what did he want? she wondered. None of this made any sense, and as soon as they reached the bedroom and he'd shut the door she drew herself up to her full height, asking coldly, "Why did you make me come here?"

"Because you could hardly share the guest room with Cynthia," he pointed out logically. "There's only the one single bed, not enough closet space——"

"I know that," Serena snapped, "and it's no real answer. I don't understand why she's here."

"You heard her. She's left Gregory."

"That's her problem," Serena countered, anger making her bold, any concern for Cynthia's problems eclipsed by the need to get her out of the guest room. "It has nothing to do with us."

"True," he conceded equitably, "but the threat of a family scandal does. Your father and Lillian refused to take her in—told her to go back to Houston."

"Fine. Let her go back to Houston."

"She refuses. She arrived with almost no money, no clothing——"

"Cynthia without any clothing?" Serena inquired scornfully, remembering her stepsister's appearance—not a wrinkle or crease to be seen. "She didn't fly in from Houston in what she's wearing now. I bet she brought plenty of stuff with her. She always does."

"Not this time. She and Gregory had a big fight this morning, and she stormed out of the house without packing a thing. After your parents refused to help her she came to my office. I talked to her and then sent her out to buy a few things to tide her over."

"Thoughtful of you," Serena scoffed, "but I still don't see why——"

"To avoid a family scandal," he repeated patiently. "If I hadn't agreed to let her come here she was going to start calling her friends—and keep calling until she found someone to take her in."

"But I still don't see——"

"You would if you gave it some thought," John pointed out reasonably. "Just imagine her, running through the pages in her address book, telling one friend after another her tale of woe."

"So what?" Serene asked recklessly. "I don't care!"

"But I do," he countered harshly, and Serena shivered, realizing that she'd finally triggered his temper. He drew her a little closer, his dark gaze impaling her, as effective at holding her captive as the grip he still had on her arm.

"I paid plenty for the privilege of becoming part of this family," he reminded her with equal parts of sarcasm and anger. "Too much to let things be spoiled by a scandal. We're going to smooth this over, put the best possible face on the situation."

"Honestly!" Serena attempted to laugh. "You sound positively medieval—as bad as my father."

"Serena, never say that again," he warned her, his dark eyes lit from within by a dangerous fire. "You may not like me, but I never sold to the highest bidder someone I claimed to love."

There was no way she could answer that; the words had pierced her, the pain more than she could bear. She turned sharply, desperate to free herself from his grip, but he held her for another moment—making it clear that his will was stronger than hers—then relented. Instantly, she was away from him, going to stand by one of the windows, resting her forehead against the cool glass.

"About Cynthia," John began again, finally breaking the heavy silence between them. "We're going to do all we can to make this look like a routine visit."

"No one will believe it," Serena responded dully, still with her back to the room—and to John. "At least no one will who knows either Cynthia or me very well."

"We'll make it clear that things are different," he countered smoothly. "Now that you're both married you have more in common. What could be more natural than that she's come to visit, to stay with you instead of your parents?"

"People know how close she and Lillian are."

"Still, now that the first..." He hesitated briefly; when he spoke again his voice was laden with sarcasm. "Now that the first blaze of our honeymoon is over, you and Cynthia naturally want to spend time together."

"I don't have the time to spend with her. I'm too busy at school," Serena reminded him, absently noting the way her breath was misting the glass. "I can't do it!"

"Of course you can. I doubt that even the great god Brandenson works as many hours a day as you do. After all you've done in the past month he can hardly refuse to give you a little time off."

So sure of himself, convinced that people will always fall in with his plans, Serena thought; so sure that I won't oppose him . . . and he's probably right. It was going to be hard to fight him every step of the way; she was already tired of living with tension, cold glances, and all the words left unspoken . . .

Behind her, he was moving about, and she found she could see his streaky reflection in the dark panes of glass. He was hunting through one of the cupboards, the one which had been hers. She'd emptied it nearly a month ago, but it looked full enough now, she noted, puzzled.

"Your things are here now," John told her—reading her mind? "When I realized Cynthia would be staying with us I called Mrs. Hutchins and told her to clear all your stuff out of the guest room."

"Why?" Serena abandoned the window to see more clearly what he was doing, watched him go through her clothes. As if he owns them—and me! she thought with a quick flare of temper which died almost as quickly as it had come. After all, he did own her, and in the most literal sense of the word. "If Cynthia brought nothing with her from Houston she won't need much space."

"I wasn't thinking of Cynthia's comfort," he corrected dispassionately. "I wanted to be sure that you and I present a united front. She's not to know how things stand between us."

"But she *does* know," Serena protested. "She's the one who told me in the first place."

"So you claimed," John allowed skeptically; he hadn't believed her the first time she'd tried to explain, and it was obvious that he still didn't. "There's nothing to say that things haven't changed between us—a month of living together in close quarters can work wonders, you know."

"You expect to convince her that we've spent the time falling madly in love?"

"That's the general idea," he agreed, a hard edge to his voice, "but I'm not going to do all the convincing. You've got to help."

"I won't!"

"You will, Serena." It sounded like a command. "It's part of the job you agreed to do, and I expect your co-operation."

"And if I refuse?"

"You'll wish you hadn't."

Period. End of discussion, she thought, shivering, preferring not to consider the means he had at his disposal to enforce his will. It was enough to know that he wouldn't hesitate to punish her. She was trapped.

"Here. Wear this." He plucked a deep rose evening dress from the closet and carried it to her. "Put it on, Serena," he ordered when she made no move to take it from him. "Put it on or, so help me, I'll do it myself."

He would, too. She knew how much pride he had; he would accept nothing less than total obedience. He was proud in a way which had nothing to do with vanity and everything to do with self-confidence, his absolute conviction that he could do anything he set his mind to. His pride had driven him to buy her, and now it seemed that even that wasn't enough. Now Cynthia was to be made to believe that what had started as a cold-blooded business arrangement had become a love match, that John Bourque had it all. And perhaps he did, Serena reflected. Certainly she had no power; to attempt to resist would simply result in another undignified skirmish, one she was sure to lose.

"All right," she said finally, reaching for the rose dress, holding it against herself like a shield, "but you'll have to leave while I change."

"Sorry, my dear——" he favored her with a slow knowing smile "—but I'm staying. I'll turn my back if you like."

"So will I," she snapped, and did so, working quickly to take off the beige suit, carelessly dropping the jacket, the skirt, and finally her blouse on the floor.

The evening dress was soft cashmere, a warm caress on her skin as she slipped into it and smoothed it into place. Before falling in graceful folds to the floor, the fabric clung lovingly—and with emphasis—to the gentle curves of her breasts...an almost wanton effect, she realized, furious with John for his choice, for making her feel that she'd been reduced to sex-object status.

"I'm ready," she announced coldly, turning to face him, coloring when she saw his lazy, appreciative smile. "Satisfied?" she demanded, and his smile broadened.

"Very much so." Slowly, he inspected her, his gaze missing nothing, lingering on the soft swell of her breasts. "Very nice, except for your hair. I want it down," he decided.

Before she could even turn toward the mirror, much less comply, he had closed the distance between them. She felt his breath stirring her hair as he began to hunt through it, his fingers gently probing, finding each hairpin and teasing it free. No! she cried silently, caught up in the anguish of memory, lacking either the courage or will to end the moment. Instead she could only stand mute before him, afraid to move, afraid even to breathe.

"There, that's better," he said when he was done, watching her face, his gaze abstracted, his fingers still threading through her hair. "You look...almost like last summer's girl," he told her, his voice deeper, the words coming more slowly, "but not quite. You need to be kissed."

"No!"

"Yes," he insisted, and, when she would have pulled away, his fingers closed on her hair, holding her firmly in place.

"You can't! You have no right."

"I have every right, sweetheart. Lord knows, I paid enough for the privilege," he coldly reminded her, but there was nothing cold in the way his mouth closed over hers, forcing her lips to part, searing them with the savagery of his intent.

At first she tried to fight him, ineffectually pushing against his shoulders, his chest. In response he deepened his kiss, increasing the pressure of his lips, his tongue exploring without restraint. There was no escape, she acknowledged bitterly, so she stood passive beneath the assault of his mouth, her hands resting uselessly on his chest. It was better to give up the fight, she tried telling herself; better not to prolong this—this assault.

But it wasn't better, she discovered in the next moment; it was infinitely worse—more dangerous. Now that she'd stopped struggling, his lips had grown softer, their pressure against hers suddenly feather light, teasing insidiously, coaxing her to respond.

She thought she'd forgotten what this could be like. She'd put behind her those hot summer nights when she'd believed that the sweet torment of his kisses meant that he loved her. It was all false—she knew that now, but the knowledge did nothing to stop her body's response. The familiar languor of desire was stealing over her, turning her bones to water. Instinctively she swayed toward him, and he instantly sensed her defeat. He released her hair to encircle her with his arms, drawing her closer as her hands stole up to grip his shoulders.

"That's right," he murmured against her mouth, gently catching her lower lip with his teeth, his embrace encouraging her to mold her pliant curves into the hard line of his body. "That's right... and about time, sweetheart," he told her, lifting his head, smiling triumphantly down at her.

"No," she protested without conviction, unsure whether she meant the word for him or herself. All she knew was that she couldn't help her response; she still craved his touch and his kiss. Already her fingers were tangling in his crisp hair, trying to draw his lips back to hers. "I hate you for this!"

"But you love how it feels," he countered, eyes alight with amusement, teasing her with brief, tempting kisses until she sighed in frustration. "One more," he promised, and his mouth finally closed over hers for a slow and leisurely exploration, creating a storm of feelings in her, inciting her to respond without reserve or restraint.

"Say what you will," he told her some indeterminate time later when the kiss had finally ended, "there's still some magic left."

"It means nothing," she told him, avoiding his gaze, furious when she heard his laughter.

"You think so? I don't, but we can settle it later. For now——" he paused to study her face "—you look properly kissed, and Cynthia's going to have a pretty good idea of what kept us."

"You took long enough," Cynthia grumbled when John and Serena returned to the living room. "I thought you'd forgotten me."

"We were tempted," John allowed dryly, directing a half smile at Serena as though the two of them were sharing a private joke, "but, as Serena's had almost nothing to eat today, we had to come down for dinner."

"I'll see what Mrs. Hutchins left for us," Serena offered, grabbing at this excuse to get away from John, even briefly. "I can——"

"No, I'll do it," he cut in smoothly. "You deserve to relax—your day's been a lot worse than mine."

Hasn't it just? Serena brooded, watching him leave the room, staring fixedly at the doorway even after he had disappeared from view.

"How domestic," Cynthia observed with a brittle laugh. "One might almost think that you'd tamed the tiger."

"What?" Serena asked blankly, trying to gather her thoughts, finding it difficult to concentrate on Cynthia after what had just happened upstairs. "Do you mean John?"

"Who else, darling?" Cynthia got up from her chair by the fire, moved gracefully to the drinks cabinet to splash whisky into her empty glass. "Do you want some?" she asked, holding the decanter aloft.

Reluctantly, Serena shook her head. A stiff drink might have helped her get through dinner, but it wasn't the wisest idea. She would need a clear head at the end of the evening, when John presumably expected her to climb those two flights of stairs to his bedroom and—— Stop! That doesn't need to be thought about now, she assured herself, making the effort to listen to Cynthia.

"Hardly seems fair," she was complaining, pausing only long enough to toss back most of her drink with reckless abandon. "Things seem to be going a lot better than you had any right to expect. You're happy——" she made it sound, Serena thought, like an accusation "—and Gregory and I have broken up!"

"Are you sure about that?" Serena had never taken Cynthia and Gregory very seriously. In her opinion, their romance and marriage had been a poor combination of infatuation and expediency; now it was just as difficult to take seriously the impending demise of that marriage. "You left Houston, but that doesn't mean you've got to get a divorce."

"But I want a divorce," Cynthia snapped. "Honestly, you sound just like John, or Mummy and Dad. I should think—after what they did to you—you'd be the last person to believe in love and marriage.''

"But things change," Serena found herself saying, because that was the kind of thing John would expect her to say. John wanted Cynthia to believe that this was a real marriage, and Serena wasn't about to openly defy him—not after that little scene in the bedroom. "Just because things started badly for us doesn't mean that we can't——" She stopped abruptly, discovering that there were, after all, limits to how far she would go to please him.

"Decide that being married to each other suits us very well," John finished for her, leaving Serena to wonder just how long he'd been standing in the doorway. "Isn't that right, love?" he inquired softly, his dark gaze holding hers, daring her to contradict.

"Yes." The word was no more than a whisper, but she managed a smile and was rewarded with an almost imperceptible nod of approval.

Damn him! she fumed, finally looking away. He'd just made it clear that he held all the aces, that she had no choice but to play the obedient wife. But when they sat down for their meal she wasn't sure why he'd bothered. At the table it was obvious that she wouldn't be called upon to play any role—at least not for a while. The conversation was all between Cynthia and John.

"I am going to get a divorce, and that's final," Cynthia defiantly announced in an opening salvo, "and I don't see why you care one way or the other."

"Because someone ought to make sure that you don't do something you're bound to regret." John was all affable charm, Serena noted, but no surprise there. He was a master at that sort of thing, at least when he wanted to be. "So long as you stay with us and give the appearance that you're just here for a visit, Gregory and his parents can pretend that everything is fine. They're not going to make the first move, and they won't forgive you if you take legal steps, or even begin to talk abou[t] problems. Bring things out in the open and your marriage is over."

"But I want it over," Cynthia insisted, launching into a long list of complaints, permitting Serena the relief of tuning out.

What happened to Cynthia's marriage was nothing to her, not when her own was such a mess! At the moment she felt consumed by the problems; for the first time in a month—since her wedding day, to be precise—she was stuck to grapple with the realities of this epic farce which bound her to John.

Ironic, she mused, that Cynthia was—however unwitting—the catalyst now. She'd served nearly the same function once before, when she'd let Serena know that, by marrying John, she was getting a business arrangement instead of the love match she'd imagined. On her wedding day, Serena's pretty fairy tale had blown up in her face—and all thanks to Cynthia....

CHAPTER TWO

CYNTHIA had tapped once on the bedroom door and then let herself in, carelessly throwing herself down on the bed. "Mummy said I ought to come and see how you're doing," she'd explained, watching Serena, who was seated at the dressing table in her creamy lace underwear, applying her makeup. "It won't be long now."

"Less than an hour," Serena had agreed evenly, brushing mascara on to her lashes.

"Don't you sound calm! I was a wreck at this point," Cynthia had recalled, sounding wistful, "but it's different for you. It must be nice..."

"What must be nice?"

"Not to have any illusions. You don't have to wonder if you'll disappoint him. I mean, all he wants is to be married to you—right? So once he's got the ring on your finger... bing! That's it, that's all he expects. You don't need to worry about keeping him happy, or doing things the way he wants them done. Just by marrying him you're home free—nothing to worry about, no need to try..." Cynthia had sighed deeply, her face unexpectedly pensive. "There are times when I wish it had been like that for Gregory and me—a nice clean business arrangement."

"...a nice clean business arrangement." A business arrangement? Serena had been listening with only half an ear, but those last few words had come through loud and clear, and were now echoing in her head. "Business arrangement?" she repeated, carefully laying aside the mascara wand. "What do you mean?"

22

"What do you mean, what do I mean?" Cynthia countered, her pensive air instantly gone, replaced by a giggle. "Renie, you know what I mean—it's so deliciously straightforward! John wants social acceptance and Daddy needs money, so Daddy lets you marry John in exchange for the money. It's all so convenient!"

Serena had been sitting with her back to Cynthia, watching her reflected image in the mirror, but now she turned to ask, "What are you talking about?"

"The deal," Cynthia responded calmly. "You know...you do know, don't you?"

"No. There's no deal," Serena said sharply, wondering why Cynthia would try to spoil her happiness by making up lies. "You know that's not true!"

"But it's what Daddy said," Cynthia protested. "I was kidding him about having been so against John at the start. I told him I didn't understand how he could suddenly be taking it so calmly, letting you marry someone with no background, no breeding...and I think I pushed him a little too far, because he finally got mad. He said that he didn't have any choice, that he was short of cash and that John had offered him so much that he couldn't refuse."

"You're lying!"

"I'm not!" Cynthia's stormy gaze tangled with Serena's. "For heaven's sake, Renie! Do you really think he's fallen in love with you? A man like that—so attractive, so deliciously physical? A man like John doesn't fall in love with a girl like you, and he certainly doesn't marry for love. John's a climber. He has to have his eye on the main chance all the time—and you're the best main chance he was ever going to get. Daddy knew that—we all knew that! You're the only one who was too blind to see... Grow up, Renie! John's not in love with you..."

And when, not caring that the wedding was now less than an hour away, Serena had gone to her father she hadn't even needed to ask. "Cynthia just tried to tell me," she'd begun, and that had been enough. The expression on her father's sleek and well-bred face had said it all. "It's true," she'd whispered, hope and happiness shriveling, dying, consumed in the conflagration that was her pain. "Daddy, I can't marry him!"

"Of course you can," he'd countered—heartily and just a shade too quickly. "This doesn't change a thing."

"It changes everything! He doesn't love me."

"But you love him," Ted Wright had put in quickly. "You want to marry him—you know you do!"

"Not now," she'd said, her voice sounding cold and dead—a stranger's voice, even to her. "Not when I know... What was it—did he want to marry into this family so badly that he offered to pay you to give your permission?"

"And if he did? What's wrong with that?"

"Everything," she whispered. "Don't you see?"

"What I see is a girl who's finally getting what she wants, and now she doesn't want it," her father blustered. "Well, I won't have it! You're crazy about him, you were determined to marry him, with or without my permission! All you've got to do is go through with the marriage. This doesn't change how you feel!"

"But it does!"

"Well, it shouldn't!" Lillian put in, speaking up for the first time. She'd been in the bedroom with Serena's father, already dressed for the wedding, very much the "but you don't look old enough to be!" stepmother of the bride. Now she moved into the argument, blue eyes blazing, not bothering to hide the cold steel of her determination. "Stop being silly, Serena. Just as your father said, you were absolutely determined to marry John, and you'll see...arranged marriages work very well, and this one will be no exception."

"There won't be a marriage," Serena insisted. "Not this way!"

"Serena, I'm afraid you don't understand," Lillian said fiercely. "You absolutely can't refuse to go through with it! John and your father have settled everything, the money gets released as soon as the wedding takes place, and your father badly needs it. Worse than that, though, if you don't marry John he'll let the whole world know——"

"Know what?" Serena demanded, looking from Lillian to her father. "What else don't I know?"

"Go ahead, Ted," Lillian commanded. "It's the only way to get her to cooperate. You've got to do it."

"Yes, I know," he agreed heavily. "Look, chick, John's offer... well, it came at the right time. I'm strapped for cash right now," he explained, appealing to reason. "The business isn't going well... some bad investments, a few irregularities... Without John's cash I could go under."

"And there's more, as if that weren't bad enough." Not missing a beat, Lillian picked up the thread. "John made your father tell him all about it. He knows everything, which is why you've got to marry him today. It's the only way to keep him silent."

"Serena, don't do this to me," her father appealed painfully, his face not so sleek now as before, gray beneath his year-round tan. "John could ruin me."

"But if——"

"There are no ifs, Serena," Lillian said flatly, she and Ted refusing to give up the fight, refusing to listen to Serena's protests, countering all her objections.

In the end they'd won, although the wedding had started late. They'd worn her down, Lillian using her autocratic will while Serena's father had traded on the debt of love she owed him. Even that, though, might not have been enough; what had finally banished the nightmare was what her father had finally said: "My dear, it's not as though John doesn't love you—at least in his fashion. Just because he's paying me, that doesn't

mean... Look, whatever you two had between you—
it's still there.''

Of course! Serena had told herself, electrified and
transformed by the thought. Why hadn't he said that in
the first place? Suddenly, everything had been made
clear. John loved her—every bit as much as she loved
him—and he hadn't been buying her name and her
family's social position. He'd given her father money in
the hope of winning his approval; John had wanted to
spare her the pain of estrangement from her family. This
wasn't a crass business arrangement—except on her
father's side. Serena did not want to examine his motives too closely, but one thing was clear: he was the one
whose hands were less than clean; he had sold his parental approval.

And John? Why, John had only been trying to make
things easy for her... of course he loved her! Instead of
wanting to call off the wedding she ought to be thanking
John—and she would, she vowed, just as soon as they
were alone!

The wedding itself had been exactly what Serena had
hoped it would be: a simple ceremony in a lovely old
church, the vows she and John exchanged charged with
deep and lasting meaning. The reception had been a different matter—something to be endured, not enjoyed.
It had been more to Lillian's taste than Serena's, although
she now understood why Lillian had worked so hard to
artfully produce such an impeccably social launch of the
marriage of her stepdaughter to a man who otherwise
wouldn't have been invited to any of Lillian's parties.
All part of the package deal John's money had bought,
Serena had told herself, wishing the two of them could
leave soon. She'd wanted—needed!—to be alone with
him. What her father had done weighed on her conscience, and the weight had seemed to grow heavier with
each passing hour.

It had begun to dawn on her that there was more to this strange business arrangement than met the eye. Even while she played the happy bride, apparently enjoying every minute of the reception, her mind was working furiously. Her father's approval had come with a price tag, one John had paid for her sake, but that didn't mean he had to like the idea! If her father hadn't been so dead set against John in the first place there would have been no question of money. Because of her father's opposition, John had been forced to pay—a bizarre form of blackmail in Serena's opinion. She was haunted by the thought that he might bitterly resent what he'd had to do, which made it imperative that she clear the air as soon as possible—as soon as they were alone!

They hadn't planned a honeymoon. For her doctorate in American Studies Serena carried a heavy load of classes, research, and work as the assistant to the head of the program; three days was all she could take off. As a consequence she and John had agreed to spend their precious little time in the little house on Birch Court. "Why waste time traveling? If we stay home we can have two days of being lazy, of doing exactly as we please," John had suggested, his glittering gaze and knowing smile making Serena's breath catch in anticipation. It had sounded perfect at the time; it would be perfect! she assured herself when the reception was behind them and they were finally home. All that was left was to put this one unfortunate detail behind them.

"John," she began—no time like the present!—as soon as he had closed the door, "there's something I want to say... about my father, what he did... Well, I just wanted to thank you."

"Did you?" She'd expected him to follow her into the living room; instead he stayed where he was, leaning against the front door, hands deep in the pockets of his pants.

As his silence lengthened she grasped the fact that he wasn't going to make this easy for her. The next step was completely up to her, and it was going to be harder than she'd thought. "It was good of you..." She hesitated, drawing a deep breath, wishing that his features weren't quite so devoid of all expression, giving her no clue as to what he was thinking. "I suppose you did it to spare my feelings, but you didn't need to."

"No?"

"Of course not. I wish he hadn't done it—I'm sorry," she offered tentatively, and then, confronting still more silence, she hurried on. "He shouldn't have, and the more I think about it, the more it seems like a put-up job...that he may have planned the whole thing..."

"You think so?" John inquired, sounding mildly amused—but also somehow detached, Serena thought, and wondered what that meant. "Are you trying to tell me you don't know for sure?"

"Yes! I had no idea. He..." This wasn't good, Serena acknowledged with a sinking feeling. John didn't sound angry, but she knew he was, and it seemed that his anger was directed at her—which made no sense. Surely he knew that the whole business had been between him and her father...so why was she getting the distinct feeling that he blamed her? "I suppose he didn't want to bother me with the details," she managed, then realized that what she'd said didn't sound quite right. "I didn't know...I wouldn't have if Cynthia hadn't told me."

"Really?" He studied her, his gaze briefly shifting, noting the way she was nervously fingering her wedding ring, then returning to her face. "You're saying that she knew more about your father's terms than you did? That, my dear, seems hard to believe."

"But it's true! I didn't even know there were terms."

"Of course you knew there were terms, and you knew that I'd accepted them—how else to explain your father's about-face?"

"I thought——" She stopped, fighting the painful lump in her throat. At the time she hadn't even tried to explain her father's sudden capitulation. She'd been too deliriously happy, relieved that there would be no more scenes, to give any thought to what had brought about the miraculous change. "I suppose...I just assumed that he wanted me to be happy."

"And until he relented you'd been so desperately unhappy—or so you had me think."

"I—you..." What was happening? she wondered, fighting a rising sense of panic. Was he accusing her? "You thought I was pretending?" she asked, incredulous.

"And still are," he told her, "although it's beyond me why you should bother now. You pulled it off—your father got what he wanted...why keep on with the act?"

"What act?" she asked with as much dignity as she could muster, determined to maintain her poise. "There wasn't any act."

"Of course there was," he contradicted softly. "You set me up, sweetheart—your distress when Daddy played his outraged-father scene, the heartrending moment when you pleaded with me to give him more time to come around..."

"I didn't plead—not really," she countered unsteadily, "and that was true. I just wanted to avoid another scene. John——" she held her hands out in a mute gesture of appeal "—it was not an act."

"All an act," he corrected carelessly, but there was a new and dangerous glitter in his eyes. This was a side of him she'd never seen before, a cruel and ruthless side. Instinctively she braced herself, waiting for the blow she knew was on the way. "You played your role—and very well—right from the start."

"That's not true," she tried one last time, but she didn't think he heard. He didn't want to hear. "Then why did you marry me?" she demanded, her voice rising, despair and anger driving her to a reckless extreme. "If you already knew all this—what a terrible person I am— why on earth did you go through with the wedding?"

"Why else?" he quizzed, finally stirring, withdrawing his hands from his pockets, taking one step toward her. "He and I got what we both wanted out of this arrangement. He got the money he needed, and I got what money usually can't buy—I've been allowed to marry into the family with his blessing. That's no small thing. It must be worth every penny I paid. I'm an insider now. I belong! Proper Boston is never going to close its doors to me again."

"Is that so important?" she raged. "Does it really matter to you?"

"What do you think?" he asked unpleasantly, taking another step toward her, forcing her to retreat. "Why else would I marry you?"

Why else, indeed? she asked herself, defeated. She should have known that from the start. A man like John didn't marry for love; he married for advancement, to improve his social standing—what had, in the old days, been called dynastic considerations. There was no love here and never had been—except what she felt for him... *had* felt, she corrected quickly, steeling herself against the pain of admitting the truth. No love... no love at all...

"What? I'm sorry," she offered automatically when she realized that someone had spoken to her, asking her a question, she thought. John and Cynthia were both watching her, finished with their meal, Serena saw, while hers was still nearly untouched. "I was thinking...miles away."

"I asked how your conference went," John prompted.

"Well enough, I suppose," she answered carefully, trying for a normality she didn't feel. "Just like any other, but interesting."

"And your paper?" John persisted, explaining to Cynthia, "Serena had a paper to present—the survey of gravestones she did this past summer...the one which brought us together," he added softly as he turned back to Serena, pretending to smile for her alone. "Was it well received?"

"I——" How did he know? she asked herself, staring fixedly down at her plate. It wasn't as though she'd discussed the conference or the paper with him; they hadn't, during this last month, discussed anything of substance. So how did he know, unless...? She kept all her work in the study across the landing from her bedroom. Her paper and the information about the conference would have been there for him to look at at any time he pleased...which is what he must have done, she decided, feeling invaded, her defense mechanism of privacy—of solitariness—suddenly destroyed. Involuntarily she looked up to meet his gaze, saw confirmation of her thoughts and a demand. He was expecting her to play the game again, compelling her to summon her reserves. "Yes, it went well, I think. There were some nice comments..."

"But you're too tired to think about it now—dead on your feet. What you need is a good night's sleep," John decided. "Go off to bed, darling. Cynthia can help me clear the table, and we won't be long."

"Not too long," Cynthia qualified with a quick sideways glance at John before she looked at Serena. "I may keep your husband up for just a little while. It's the novelty," she explained with a pretty smile. "I'd like to spend some time with him...now that I know he's not the dreadful man Mummy always said he was. You won't mind, will you?"

"Of course not." No, she didn't mind, Serena mused as she left the room; in fact, she didn't care if the two of them stayed up all night! What she did mind was the way she'd been dismissed, sent off to bed—like a child, she thought resentfully, pausing halfway up the first flight of stairs.

"Coffee?" she heard John ask, all affable charm, heard Cynthia's lilting laugh before she said,

"Why not, but in the living room, by the fire...so much more cozy, don't you think?"

Very cozy! Serena thought waspishly, continuing on up the stairs. She was willing to bet that John would be smiling now, his eyes lit with that knowing amusement she'd seen far too often. They were two of a kind, she fumed, reaching the first landing, forgetting John and Cynthia when it suddenly occurred to her that she had a pressing problem. Where was she going to sleep?

She knew what John expected, but, after that scene before dinner, did he seriously believe that she would willingly go back to his bedroom? Of course he did, she acknowledged bleakly, and what choice did she have? Cynthia was in the guest room, and Mrs. Hutchins had moved Serena's things upstairs... Everything? she wondered, staring at the closed guest-room door in morbid fascination. Cynthia and John were still talking; Serena could not make out their words, but she could hear them—confidential, even intimate. Time enough for a quick look, she assured herself, silently opening the door.

Typically, Cynthia had left on every light, and Serena had no trouble seeing how much the room had changed. The highly polished surfaces of the bureau and dressing table had been swept clear of her things; her stack of books was gone from the table beside the bed. If she checked the cupboard or opened any of the drawers she knew she'd find that nothing of hers had been left behind.

Now Cynthia was clearly in possession: a profusion of boxes and bags from Newbury Street's smart boutiques were scattered around the room, a couple open and empty, drifts of pastel tissue paper on the floor— the fruits of a busy afternoon. Cynthia was a dedicated shopper, never more so than when someone else was picking up the tab—as John assuredly was this time. Paying her family's bills, Serena mused, was getting to be a habit—a thought which forcibly recalled her to the present.

He'd paid enough to demand her obedience; she didn't like to think what kind of scene he'd make if she attempted to reclaim this room. Besides, everything of hers was one flight up, in John's bedroom...which was where she'd better go, she told herself. She had no choice—no choice at all—and her hands were suddenly cold and not quite steady when she pulled shut the door to the room which had been her refuge for the last few weeks.

She would have to sleep in John's room. Cynthia's presence in the little house had put Serena completely at his mercy—an advantage he had no doubt recognized almost as soon as Cynthia had appeared in his office. John was a great one for seeing possibilities and making events work for him, Serena knew. Without that ability, he wouldn't have come so far, accomplished so much; it worked for him in business, it had worked for him with her.

And now he had her exactly where he wanted her, Serena acknowledged, fighting a hard knot of fear as she stepped across the threshold of his room. She closed the door behind her, wishing for a key, wanting to lock him out. If only she could! she brooded. Let him work out where to spend the night—with Cynthia, for all she cared! Instead—and Serena had to force herself to accept the grim reality—he would spend the night here, with her.

Once, before she'd learned the truth and her dreams had been destroyed, she had wanted to share this room with John, had thought it the most beautiful room in the world. She had actually been counting the days until——

No! Don't remember that, she urged herself, switching on one dim light before lowering herself into the bentwood rocking chair, staring fixedly at the large four-poster bed. She bit her lip, remembering how she'd responded earlier when John had kissed her. If she shared the bed with him tonight, and if he touched her...she was afraid she knew what would happen. She'd betray herself again, and this time would be worse.

"No!" She spoke aloud, and the word came out as a strangled whisper. She wouldn't let that happen again. She would stiffen her resolve, preserve some small part of herself for herself. She could not—would not!—let him destroy the last of her pride. But how? she asked herself, leaning back and closing her eyes. There was no love between them, but there was—well, chemistry, she decided, for lack of a better word...chemistry working on her.

And John? Did the chemistry work on him too? She couldn't be sure. It was hard to believe that he desired her. She wasn't his type: she was too normal. A man like John would have grown accustomed to exotic women, intensely exciting women... He couldn't possibly want her—not really! For him it was probably just a matter of pride. Did he, she wondered, want to humiliate her? Did this whole class thing run so deep with him that he resented her for having been born with the advantages he lacked? Would forcing himself on her make him feel superior or feel that he'd balanced the scales in some strange way?

Put like that, Serena reflected, it sounded ridiculous, too melodramatic for words, but she couldn't know how much social acceptance meant to him. She'd been one of the elect since birth—not that she'd ever cared. But, as Lillian—whose own hold on status had once been precarious—was fond of saying, the only people who didn't care about status were those born with it. Did John really care that much? Serena wondered. It was hard to believe of someone that capable, that self-assured, that successful, but she couldn't know what insults and snubs he'd been forced to endure as he had made his way up the ladder of business success. Still, there were bound to have been plenty. Back when they'd started seeing each other, hadn't she tried to keep him away from Lillian and her father? But only to spare him, Serena assured herself, because she'd known they wouldn't approve. They would have made cutting remarks—and all because John didn't have the "right" background... The snob factor at work, and who knew its power? It had driven John into this marriage, hadn't it?

So what? she asked herself, realizing just how far her thoughts had drifted. Thinking about John's need for acceptance had accomplished nothing—except to make her view him in a slightly more sympathetic light, and she didn't need that! Instead, she should be deciding how to handle the end of this evening, how to keep him at a distance—anything to avoid sharing the bed with him!

Perhaps... the narrow day bed in the dressing room? Remembering it brought a quick flare of hope, one instantly cut off when she heard sounds of movement in the house—the deep, indistinct tones of John's voice, the clear lilt of Cynthia's laughter, the creak of a stair tread.

"Still up?" John inquired pleasantly as he entered the room. "I thought you'd be sound asleep by now."

"No." It might have been better if she'd pretended to be, she reflected, but it was too late for that now. "I was——"

"Waiting for me?" he inserted smoothly, closing the door and then leaning against it, watching her. "I wish I'd known."

"You know damn well I wasn't waiting for you," she flared. "I was trying to decide where to sleep."

"You'll sleep here——" he spoke softly, but there was a world of resolve behind his words "—where you belong."

"Not with you!"

"So you've said before," he agreed equitably, subjecting her to that brief knowing smile. "So what's the problem?"

"I won't..." she tried to swallow, wishing that her throat wasn't so dry "...that is, you can't...I won't let you..."

"What? Have my way with you?" he supplied for her, his tone still deceptively mild. "Don't worry, sweetheart, I have no intention of forcing the issue. I'm waiting for you to make the first move."

"Which I'll never do," she snapped, finding courage in anger. "You'll wait until hell freezes over!"

"You think so?" He left the door, closing the distance between them to smile down at her upturned and flushed face. "I don't, not after that brief encounter we had earlier. You gave yourself away, Serena."

"It won't happen again," she promised, forcing herself to meet the challenge in his dark eyes. "You bought my name and my background, my place in your house——"

"And in my bed," he put in softly.

"—and whatever social acceptance my father and Lillian can pass on," she continued doggedly, ignoring his comment, "but you didn't buy me. You can't have me, not that part anyway."

"And yet, back in the summer," he mused, his voice shaded as though by pleasant remembering, "you certainly seemed to be offering that part of yourself."

"That was before," she protested, a wave of color scalding her cheeks, "before I knew——"

"That I'd taken the bait? That you and your sainted father had pulled off the scheme?"

"Before I knew that all you wanted was to buy me," she corrected, her anger rising again.

"So you've told me—not that it matters..." He leaned toward her, his fingers lightly brushing across her burning cheek. "There's too much attraction between us, Serena Winslow Wright Bourque. No matter how much you protest, it's going to happen...but not tonight. I want you to be rested—enthusiastic—when we make love for the first time."

"Ha! Don't you just wish——?"

"Yes," he agreed shortly, giving her a brief glimpse of his twisted expression before he turned away toward the windows. "Why don't you use the bathroom first," he said after a moment, "and then you'll sleep in here? I'll take the couch in the dressing room...unless you change your mind."

Never! she vowed, but silently. The last thing she wanted was to keep this fight going until she goaded him into something she'd regret for the rest of her life. Better now to do as he said, so she hunted up a nightgown and robe, then made her way through the dressing room, into the bathroom.

When she returned he was still facing the windows, apparently absorbed by the cold rain streaking the glass. Warily, she circled around his brooding, enigmatic presence and slipped into bed. "Will you leave now?" she asked tentatively.

"Of course." He nodded, abandoning his study of the window to switch off the one lamp. "Good night, Serena," he said into the darkness.

His footsteps retreated, then the dressing room door closed behind him and Serena finally released the breath she'd unconsciously been holding. She could still hear him, though, moving around the small dressing room and then the bathroom, until the beat of the shower finally covered any other noise.

The steady sound should have lulled her to sleep, but the novelty of knowing that he was so near was disturbing. So was the bed, Serena discovered, restlessly turning, punching up one pillow, then another, trying to find a position to please her. It was hopeless, she finally decided. This bed was too large and luxurious, too much of a change from the small single one she'd been using... the one Cynthia was using tonight.

Damn Cynthia, Serena thought, staring into the darkness. If Cynthia hadn't left Gregory none of this would have happened—not being here in this bed, not this new and confrontational relationship with John... It was all Cynthia's fault!

Which wasn't a terribly worthy thought, Serena reflected. It made her sound childish, unwilling to take responsibility for a mess that wasn't Cynthia's doing. Cynthia's unexpected arrival really hadn't had that much effect. Perhaps it had hurried certain inevitabilities, but Serena realized now what she ought to have known from the start—that sooner or later John would have forced the issue between them. She couldn't blame Cynthia for that, and it seemed silly to be angry with her, particularly at this late date.

They'd never fought much as children, a fact which had pleased their father no end. When he'd married Lillian, bringing her and Cynthia into his home, he'd been determined to create a happy family—a real family. Against the odds, that was exactly what had happened. Young as she was, Serena had known that she had almost nothing in common with her stepmother or Cynthia. They cared about appearances—the right clothes, hairstyles, parties, friends—while Serena was already a bookworm and a solitary soul, happiest in the private world of her imagination. She and Cynthia had gone their separate ways, and Lillian had found that she'd needed to exert only minimal parental control over the child of her husband's first marriage. There had been few arguments and none of the bitter scenes which often marred attempts to merge a child of a first marriage into a second.

By the time Serena entered her teen years she had known that the social scene—all-important to Lillian and Cynthia—wasn't for her. She'd withdrawn from the field of combat to concentrate on her studies. Privately, she'd thought it was ridiculous to spend so much time on what was socially correct. She'd probably been, Serena could admit now, something of a reverse snob, convinced that she was a superior being. Still, she'd been tactful, hiding her disdain of social status and her conviction that she was above that sort of thing.

She supposed, though, that her attitude explained why she had rejected any suggestion that John was less than perfect. If anything, Lillian's opinion had worked in reverse, practically driving Serena into his arms, she reflected, lying in the darkness, remembering . . .

CHAPTER THREE

"YOU'RE going to see that dreadful man now, I suppose." Lillian had glanced up over the tortoiseshell frames of her half glasses, regarding Serena with ill-concealed displeasure. "I wish you wouldn't. He's only after an invitation to our party."

Not "our party," Serena mentally corrected; leave me out of this! It's *your* party; yours and Cynthia's. The two of them were sitting together at the pretty little gate-leg table which served as Lillian's desk. They were both very fair, although Serena suspected that a hairdresser was now responsible for at least some of the golden highlights in Lillian's hair. Mother and daughter had the same light blue eyes, the same delicate profiles, the same diminutive but nicely rounded figures, the same brilliant smiles. "We're alike enough to be sisters," Lillian was fond of pointing out, and it was true. While Cynthia had been growing up, Lillian had managed to pretty well stop the clock on herself, so that the two of them now appeared to be the same indeterminate age.

Two of a kind in every way, Serena thought, and not even Cynthia's marriage the previous year had affected the close relationship between mother and daughter. Ostensibly, Cynthia lived in Houston now, but she was home for the summer, working with Lillian on plans for the Fourth of July party they held each year at the family's summer place, south of Boston.

The same old routine, Serena told herself; nothing had changed. There were the same endless discussions about the invitation list—who's in? Who's out? Which really big social figures can we get to come? When they finally got the list settled she knew they'd spend even more endless hours agonizing over the food—was boiled lobster still the in thing, or should they go for something clever? Would a catered clambake be too showy? All those meaningless decisions to make, Serena thought with her old feeling of superiority. Thank goodness she didn't care about that sort of thing!

"Why don't you wait until after the Fourth?" Lillian suggested, filling the vacuum created by her step-daughter's silence. "It's only a couple of weeks, and I don't want that man embarrassing our friends, trying to ingratiate himself."

"Who?" Cynthia asked, looking up from her list for the first time.

"That dreadful man," Lillian said again. "John Bourque. The developer who's trying to buy his way into the parties that count...you know! No, you don't," she realized, favoring Cynthia with a sympathetic smile. "By the time he began to push his way in you were so mad about Gregory that you weren't paying attention. He's an outsider, a climber, utterly no background! He'd just love to get in with us, and I wouldn't put it past him to have bought the place next to this just so we'd be his nearest neighbors in the summer."

"I think you're overrating us," Serena put in dryly, and was instantly subjected to Lillian's best icy cold stare, the one she used in place of angry words.

Easy for you to say; the unspoken reproach hung in the air. "Do you?" Lillian gathered her poise to ask. "I don't. We're exactly the sort of people he wants to accept him. Put him off, dear."

"I can't," Serena objected mildly. "We have an appointment."

"That needn't matter," Lillian countered. "You could call and tell him it's too hot to come out today."

"Not as hot as Houston," Cynthia put in fretfully, seizing the opportunity to launch into her litany of complaints—Houston was too hot, too damp, too big, too new, but the bottom line was that Houston wasn't Boston. Privately, Serena suspected that the real problem was Gregory, that he was proving to be not quite as exciting as Cynthia had expected, but any discussion of that sensitive subject took place when she and her mother were alone. In public, Gregory wasn't mentioned; Cynthia concentrated on Houston's deficiencies, playing to Lillian's patient listening and sympathetic responses.

But not this time, Serena noted. Lillian didn't want to hear about Houston; it was interrupting her campaign to keep Serena from going to see John Bourque. Briefly, Cynthia was subjected to her mother's best blue ice-chip stare. "Darling, I know Houston's terribly hot, but it can't be much worse than this, and it is a way for Serena to break this appointment of hers."

"You'd better find some way to get out of it," Cynthia advised, flashing Serena a conspiratorial smile. "Mummy won't let you hear the end of it if you don't."

"Listen, I am not going to ask this man to the party," Serena promised. "All I want is a quick look at the graveyard that happens to be on his land."

Lillian rolled her eyes heavenward, then said darkly, "It's too much of a coincidence that he agreed to show you his dreary little graveyard just two weeks before the Fourth. He's obviously fishing for an invitation, but I won't have him at my party!"

"Fine. I won't ask him." Tired of the argument and anxious to end it, Serena gathered up her keys and the tote bag packed with her supplies, then turned on her heel and left the house.

If only she hadn't decided to sublet her apartment to spend the summer down here, Serena brooded when she was alone in her car. At the time the idea had seemed to make perfect sense: living rent-free at the summer place, plus the sublet income, would do wonders for her savings, and she'd need every cent if she got the appointment as Professor Brandenson's teaching assistant—lots of prestige, but not much money. When Serena had made her plans they'd seemed ideal; besides saving money, living at the summer place would make it easy to do some solid research—a survey of the colonial graveyards in this small coastal town.

Ideal! she thought, shaking her head; more fool you! Still, it would have worked if only Cynthia hadn't unexpectedly come back for the summer. Without Cynthia here Lillian would have spent most of her time at the house in Boston. Serena wouldn't have seen much of anyone, except for the few days before the Fourth of July party. Once that manic gaiety and confusion had ended, Serena would have had the house to herself. But Cynthia, unexpectedly back from Houston, hadn't wanted to stay in Boston. She and Lillian had settled into the cramped summer place, bringing constant confusion with them, and forcibly reminding Serena of the social games she'd long since decided to avoid.

Oh, stop it! she advised herself now, finally starting her battered little car and reversing down the drive. All this brooding was pointless, and she was about to be late for her appointment with John Bourque—the social climber, if Lillian could be believed, and she probably could. After all, Lillian knew almost everything there was to know about Boston society, while Serena had been out of touch for several years.

As a consequence, she knew almost nothing about John Bourque, except that he had become an important force in Boston, responsible for many of the new office and residential towers rising on the skyline. Because she didn't move in Lillian's world of glittering charity benefits, Serena had never laid eyes on the man. Perhaps he was a climber, but he was nothing to her. Lillian's dark imaginings to the contrary, Serena told herself with a wry smile, John Bourque would have to do his climbing without any help from her.

All she wanted from him was a chance for a few hours alone in the little abandoned burial ground which occupied one small corner of his considerable property. She needed to record the words on the old gravestones, make some notes about what carvers had made the stones. She might take a few photographs or perhaps make a rubbing or two. That was all there was to it; no need for Lillian to concern herself. Serena would spend a few minutes with John Bourque, a few hours on his land, and that would be that—or so she thought until she saw him for the first time.

For a moment she'd thought she'd been forgotten— that should please Lillian, she'd told herself, repressing a nervous giggle. She'd knocked repeatedly on the imposing front door, finally giving up to search for another entrance. There didn't seem to be one, but when she'd worked her way around to the back she found that the three wings of the house created a sheltered and brilliantly sunny courtyard, complete with swimming pool, a few rattan chairs and a couple of sun loungers.

On one of them was a man. And what a man! she thought, her heart leaping as she stared in fascination at the sleek and powerful teak brown form. He was wearing cutoff jeans—nothing else, not even a shirt— and his back was to her, which gave her the opportunity to admire this impressively large and well-muscled man.

Then, as though sensing her presence, he turned, muscles rippling beneath that dark golden skin, and his gaze connected with hers. It was only a small moment, but for Serena it was everything—enough to stir something within her...something she'd never imagined or experienced before, something which must have been lying dormant, waiting for John Bourque's awakening presence in her life...

Sexual attraction, Serena told herself, sitting up in the bed, all hope of getting to sleep gone now. What she'd experienced when she'd first met John was sexual attraction—nothing more.

Nothing more? She repressed a nervous laugh, drawing up her legs, linking her arms around them, resting her forehead on her knees. Nothing more than sexual attraction was plenty! It was more than enough for someone as inexperienced as she'd been ... and still was, she acknowledged. The only change in her was that she now understood the power of sexual attraction, knew what desire could do.

Her family's disapproval had driven her into John's orbit, but sexual attraction—the sheer power of his magnetic physical presence—had kept her there. It had happened in only an instant; her safe and careful little world had come tumbling down when she'd found him by the pool. In that brief moment before he'd sensed her presence she'd already been lost, possessed by emotions completely new to her.

She had wanted to touch him, she remembered now. She had stood frozen in place, wondering what it would be like to feel the power beneath the flesh, to measure the breadth of those shoulders, to savor the heat she knew would be there ... Her throat suddenly dry, both hands clutching the handles of her tote bag, she had watched John Bourque swing one leg over the lounger, bending to slip his bare feet into battered running shoes then straightening to reach for a blue knit shirt. He'd pulled it on with brief economy, ruffling his dark hair into casual disorder.

When he stood up, finally turning toward her, she saw that he was very tall, lean and hard, every movement sensuous grace as he tucked his shirt into the waistband of his shorts. His eyes, she saw, were pools of darkness, and his mouth curved slightly at one corner, as though something—the warmth of the sun, perhaps—pleased him. When he started toward her she was forcibly reminded. of a jungle cat, something sleek and powerful, in control and in command.

"I'm John Bourque," he announced, extending his hand, holding hers briefly in his firm grip, leaving her feeling oddly bereft when he released her. "Why don't we sit down?" He gestured toward a shaded corner, waiting until she was seated before taking the chair opposite hers.

"So——" he paused, eyeing her without pretense: first her face, then assessing her modest curves '—Serena Winslow Wright." He continued when he'd completed his inspection, his gaze now holding hers, "Age: twenty-five; occupation: student." When he saw her puzzled expression he treated her to a brief flashing smile, even white teeth very pronounced against his deep tan. "When I got your letter I looked you up in the city directory," he explained easily. "That's one thing you'll learn about me. I'm thorough. I don't miss much."

He wouldn't, Serena realized, spellbound. Lillian would mutter darkly if she learned what this man had done; "Checking your background, wanting to be sure that you were who he thought, that you could be useful to him," Lillian would say—but that was Lillian's paranoia, and Serena chose not to believe her.

Which had been foolish—inevitable, perhaps, but still foolish—she reflected now, lying down again, curling up in the huge bed, determined to get some sleep. Perhaps...if anyone but Lillian had said those things, Serena mused, would she have listened? Probably not. She suspected that, by the end of that first afternoon, it had already been too late...

"Tell me why you want to see my graveyard," John Bourque had commanded. "Your letter said that you're a graduate student in American Studies, but—what does that mean exactly?"

"I'm studying very early New England—the people, how they lived, their work, their architecture, their religious beliefs—and the largest collection of Puritan artifacts we have are their gravestones. What I'm doing now is a survey of the small graveyards here in town.'' She paused briefly, because this man—with his physical splendor and almost palpable energy—threatened to rob her of her powers of concentration; it was an effort to focus on the dry details of her study. "I'm looking at the work of the various eighteenth-century carvers, hoping to learn which families favored which carvers, how the images carved reflect their beliefs.''

"Sounds complicated.''

"Not really. Not if..."

"Not if you know your stuff," he finished for her, correctly guessing what she'd intended to say when she'd trailed off in embarrassment. "If it's true—and it obviously is in your case—why not say so?''

"Well..." she hesitated, disconcerted by his directness "...if I did it would sound——"

"Realistic," he supplied firmly. "Why hide your light under a bushel?''

Certainly he never would, Serena knew. He couldn't. His abilities, his accomplishments were tangible—huge buildings rising on the Boston skyline. He was a man who could do great things, and he looked the part. He wasn't like her—depressingly average. He did large and exciting things, while she poked around in lonely, forgotten old graveyards—a morbid thought!

"But you didn't come here to listen to my opinion of you," he said quietly, interrupting her train of thought. "You came to see my graveyard." He stood up, a lithe and catlike movement. "Shall we go?''

Serena hadn't expected him to come with her; had it been anyone but John Bourque she would have preferred to be left alone. Even now, in her twenties, she still felt awkward and self-conscious in the presence of any man she didn't know well—and with good reason.

She was a studious girl who hadn't done much dating, and her field of study didn't help. Few men wanted to talk to a girl who had buried herself in the past!

Left alone, she was happily unselfconscious, so absorbed in what she was learning that she forgot her shyness. Under normal circumstances she would have welcomed the hours alone in John Bourque's graveyard, would have preferred not to have his company...but these weren't normal circumstances! she assured herself, her spirits soaring. There was nothing normal about John Bourque, nothing normal about how he made her feel when he looked at her.

Incredibly, he appeared to like her; even more incredibly, he seemed to find her attractive! He was doing wonders for her morale, and she welcomed his presence. Unexpectedly, what should have been just another afternoon's work—another old graveyard to study—had become something magical, even enchanted.

"It's in pretty bad shape," he offered apologetically when they'd reached the tumbled remnant of the stone wall which encircled the burial ground.

Standing together, they surveyed the wild overgrowth: tall grass, brush and brambles, a couple of gnarled and undisciplined climbing roses. Only a few of the tallest slate markers were visible through the tangle, their soft gray a calm counterpoint to the greenery which surrounded them.

"It's wonderful," Serena said, her voice hushed to avoid breaking the spell. "I think it's gorgeous."

"Do you?" he asked with a quick slanting smile. "Most people wouldn't."

"I know," she agreed happily, discovering that she didn't mind if this man thought she was different, "but I'm not like most people."

"Certainly not. You're unique," he assured her, "unworldly, one of life's innocents...refreshingly so." He offered his hand—his sure, strong grip, she thought, savoring the brief contact between them—to help her over the stone wall.

Once inside he let her lead, but as soon as she knelt to inspect the first marker he was there, bending to hold the tall grass away. She shyly smiled her thanks, then quickly turned to study the details carved in the stone.

"A winged skull—one of the North River carvers," she noted, thinking out loud, running her hand over the hard textured slate. "A nice stone, well preserved, but nothing special..."

She'd hoped for more, she acknowledged, moving on to the next stone, where John Bourque again parted the tall grass which hid the stone's details. She'd been expecting something exciting, a real find. Anything had seemed possible because of John's presence, because he—well, he was an exciting man, wasn't he? Exciting, attractive, so much nicer than he needed to be, intensely male...and she was staring at his hands, she realized—strong hands, well-kept but nothing soft about them, long slender fingers... Alarmed at the track her thoughts were taking, she forced herself—finally!—to look at the stone.

"Yes," she whispered, her breath catching. Here was what she'd been hoping to find, what fate seemed to have decreed she'd find on this day when she'd already discovered John Bourque. Here was the strong, beautifully incised carving, the characteristic vase with its lily and wreath of foliage, the borders decorated with more lilies...there was no doubt! "It's a JN," she announced, triumphant, looking up at John, laughing out loud at the sheer joy of having made the discovery. "No one knew it was here, and I found it! You can't imagine how that makes me feel!"

"That's right, I can't," he agreed, his gaze fixed on her face, "but it must be good."

"Better than good! He's my favorite carver, and...
perhaps there are more," she added breathlessly, pre-
paring to stand up again.

"I hope so," he told her, his voice indulgent, offering
his hand, its pressure on hers briefly increasing. "Does
this mean that my burial ground pleases you?"

"Oh, it does," she assured him, off to look at the rest
of the stones the moment he released her, moving lightly,
almost dancing from one to the next.

There were two more stones carved by JN—in this one
little graveyard! she marveled when she'd finished her
first brief inspection. "Now, there's so much to do..."
She turned, wondering where she'd abandoned her tote
bag, recalled to the present when she nearly collided with
John Bourque. "I'm sorry! I forgot you were here," she
apologized artlessly.

"That's all right," he assured her with a lazy, heart-
stopping smile, "just so long as you don't make me
leave."

"Make you leave?" she repeated wonderingly. "It's
your graveyard, Mr. Bourque——"

"John," he corrected, still smiling at her, "and it's
yours now, for as long as you like."

"It could take hours," she warned, and it did, but he
stayed with her, and never gave any indication that he
was bored.

"There, I'm done," she finally announced when she'd
completed her work—at least as much of it as it was
practical to do in one day. For the benefit of the tall,
silent figure beside her, she smiled brightly—too brightly,
she knew. She didn't want to be finished, didn't want
this afternoon's magic to end. She couldn't remember
when she'd been quite so happy—it wasn't every day
that she found three previously unknown JN stones...
and John Bourque, a small voice inside her head
prompted, and she knew that he was the real reason she
wanted this afternoon to go on and on.

Which is stupid! she lectured herself. She was wishing for something completely beyond her grasp; John Bourque wasn't really interested in her. Just because he'd been polite and hadn't made her feel totally gauche, she was letting her imagination run wild, wanting something she couldn't have.

"I must go now," she said, hoping he wouldn't be able to tell how much the words cost her.

"If you insist." He nodded, turning to lead the way, breaking a path through the undergrowth.

"If you don't mind I'd like to come back one more time," she told him, carefully skirting a wild tangle of briers, "but I won't—— Ouch!" Something snagged her hair and tugged painfully at her scalp, forcing her to stand motionless. "I'm caught."

"So you are, by a climbing rose." He had already turned to look back, and now he took a few steps toward her. "I'll fix it."

He moved even closer, until there were only a few inches between them, and Serena felt as trapped by his nearness as by the thorns. Afraid to meet his eyes, she stared straight ahead, distracted by the way his knit shirt molded itself to the flat planes and hard muscles beneath, by the undeniably masculine scent of him and the heat radiating from his body. She waited, frozen in place, and when his fingers began to probe gently in her hair she inhaled sharply, an instinctive response to his touch.

"Sorry, I don't mean to hurt you," he apologized, "but you're really caught."

She closed her eyes for an instant, grateful that he hadn't guessed what she was feeling, then managed, in a small strangled voice, "That's all right."

"Better not say so before I finish the job," he advised, "if I do. These thorns have a mind of their own... Perhaps if I take out some of the pins?"

"Anything." Anything to end this madness, she told herself; anything to end the contrary mix of awareness and lassitude invading her body, anything to set her free before she succumbed to the mad impulse to place her hands on his chest, anything...before she made a complete fool of herself!

One by one he removed the pins and her hair tumbled over his hands—those strong brown hands... Briefly they stirred in her hair, then the tips of his fingers were on her scalp. She felt their pressure increasing, compelling her closer, until her forehead was on his chest, her cheeks, burning hot, against his knit shirt. She could feel the steady movement of each breath he drew...and she wanted to stay here forever! She wanted his arms around her, his lips on hers, the length of his body bending hers to his will. Madness! she tried telling herself, but the word had no meaning. The only reality left in her universe was the contact between her and this man...

"Just a bit longer," he told her, his voice a deep and intimate murmur. "You're nearly free."

But she would never be free, she realized as he continued, gently working her hair away from each thorn. For as long as she lived she would remember this moment: the lonely graveyard, the heat and the scent of roses, the sound of his quiet breathing, his touch in her hair.

I'm not in love, she assured herself; no one falls in love in a few hours! Still, given more time she had the feeling she could fall in love with John Bourque. Already, in this long moment, she'd felt something new—the magic of being close to a man, of his touch...and all because of some thorns, she mused dreamily. It felt so right—as though she'd come home, in out of the cold—and she knew that she'd stay here forever if only——

"That's the last of them." His voice broke the silence between them, but not the spell. The thorns no longer held her, but—incredibly!—he did, his fingers slowly threading through her hair. "I want to see you again," he told her, his voice and his touch both teasing at her senses. "Tonight? Will you let me take you out to dinner?"

Slightly, almost imperceptibly, she nodded, and felt him release a breath she hadn't known he was holding.

"Good." Finally he let her go, stepped back to study her face for a moment, then smiled. "About seven? Will that give you time to be ready?"

"Time to be ready...if you get up now. Otherwise you're going to be late."

It was John's voice, the deep and intimate tone like a caress, but Serena knew there was something wrong, something out of place. Reluctantly she opened her eyes and saw that the world had changed. They were no longer in the lush green of the graveyard, and John was no longer wearing the blue knit shirt she remembered. Instead, he had on something white; it appeared to be a robe, not a shirt, and it left exposed an impressive expanse of hard-muscled flesh.

But when had he changed? she wondered, closing her eyes again, trying to work out what had happened.

"Serena, wake up. This is Wednesday. Don't you have an early conference?"

The conference! Professor Brandenson's conference! The here and now hit her like a lead weight. Her eyes snapped open and she pushed herself into a sitting position. "Sorry," she began automatically. "My alarm clock...I must have forgotten."

"Not surprising, given the alterations in our arrangement, but it's not a problem." He smiled, his gaze scorching her as it left her face, drifted lower. "Waking you up is no hardship. I'll gladly do it each morning."

"That won't be necessary," she snapped, wide-awake now, snatching the sheet and drawing it up to her chin to protect herself from his careful inspection. "I'll make sure I set the alarm from now on."

"I'm sure you will," he agreed, a sarcastic edge to his voice. "Anything, I suppose, to avoid contact between us."

"That's right."

"Then I'd better make the most of what I have now," he decided, sweeping the sheet from her grasp, beginning to finger the satin straps of her nightgown.

"Don't touch me!"

"Sorry, sweetheart, but it's a bit late to defend maidenly virtue." He leaned closer, and she caught the clean male scent of him. "I've already seen—and touched—everything on display now," he reminded her, his eye lit with a dangerous spark, "and that was before I paid for the privilege." His glittering gaze held her, daring her to protest as his fingers traced down one strap, his palm lightly brushing the swell of her breast. "That gives me even more right to do as I please."

"No—it doesn't," she whispered, afraid to move, even to breathe, but knowing she had to do something to stop him. Already her pulses were racing, desire twisting itself into a hard knot of longing. He would know, she thought despairingly, he'd be able to feel her response. "John, you can't——"

"Don't tell me what I can't do," he warned, bending closer until his face was just inches from hers. "You have no say in the matter—remember? I bought you; I paid more than enough. I'm entitled to do as I please."

For a long moment he watched her, saying nothing, his hand motionless on her breast, the tension of this strange intimacy arcing between them. It was obvious that he was reading something from her expression, but he was giving away nearly as much of himself. A pulse beat furiously at his temple, and the skin was drawn taut over his features, permitting her a glimpse of the slight tinge of color beneath what remained of his summer tan.

She read anger in his expression—anger and something more complex. Her resistance had offended his pride, she guessed; in spite of the cold-blooded terms of their marriage, he was determined to make her want him. Her presence in his bed, his hand on her breast weren't enough for him. He wanted more; he would always want more—whatever it took to keep this arrangement from turning to ashes for him.

Or had it already? she wondered. Did he already hate himself for the trap he'd laid? Did he already realize that he had trapped not just her, but himself? Was he already regretting this farce of a marriage, wanting something real, something warm? Look what you've done! she grieved. Look what you've done to yourself and to me...but her anguish lasted only until he broke the silence between them, his hard edge making her flinch.

"You belong to me now," he told her. "You're my possession, and I can do whatever I please...whenever I please. Understand?"

Fractionally, she nodded.

"Good." For a moment longer their perilous world hung suspended, then he withdrew his hand and moved away from the bed, and Serena finally dared draw a breath.

If only he wasn't so deep, she brooded under the healing warmth of the shower. Complex, enigmatic ... she needed to get beyond the barriers he'd erected, needed to understand what he was thinking and feeling. If she could do that there might be a——

Might be what? A chance? she asked herself, the sensible part of her mind taking over, facing reality for her. Understanding John wouldn't help. He didn't want love; it was pointless to try to go back, to make last summer's dreams a reality. Those dreams were gone...and so was the girl she had been when she'd thought they were in love.

She knew better now. Perhaps she had loved John for a while, but that was over! How could she love him after what he had done to her? He was one of life's users, too shrewd and calculating to make room for love in his life. She couldn't possibly love a man like that!

"No, of course not," Serena said dully, closing her eyes against the threat of tears, hating the clever, disbelieving, sensible part of herself. Once, back in the summer, she had thought she was done with that part of herself. She had gladly relinquished control, had lived on emotion and let her heart dictate her decisions.

What a mistake! she acknowledged sadly, reaching out blindly to switch off the shower, standing motionless while the last drops of water gathered themselves to course slowly—almost sensually—down her tingling skin. Last summer had been a form of madness; she was over it now, but still at John's mercy... 'I can do whatever I please...whenever I please," he had threatened, and she shivered, suddenly cold.

She stepped out of the shower, wrapping one towel around her wet hair and using a larger one to dry herself, finally letting it serve for a robe, cinched just above the swell of her breasts. Barefoot, she padded back to the bedroom, stopping dead just inside the door when she saw John. He was dressed now—every inch the proper Bostonian in a well-tailored pinstripe suit, crisp white shirt, and discreetly patterned silk tie.

"I brought up some coffee," he said blandly, ignoring her outraged expression. "Would you like some?"

"I don't have time." She stood motionless, pointedly waiting for him to leave. "I've got to dress and do my hair."

"Don't let me stop you."

But he had. There was no way she was going to strip off the towel and dress while he watched; he knew it and was amused. Damn him! she fumed, deliberately turning her back to rummage through the drawers of the dressing table until she found where Mrs. Hutchins had put her blow dryer. When she raised her head she found his reflected image in the oval mirror, and her defiant gaze locked with his more speculative one. "Do you enjoy invading my space?" she demanded.

"That's such a cliché," he chided gently. "I suppose the women's magazines are full of jargon like that, but I expect better of you."

"Sorry to have disappointed you."

"No, you haven't done that," he told her, watching as she pulled the towel from her hair. "Exasperated me, perhaps, and frustrated me...yes, you have frustrated me, but..."

She didn't need to listen to this, she decided, switching on the blow dryer to drown out his words.

In the mirror, his reflection reached over her shoulder, taking the dryer from her hand and switching it off. "Not yet, Serena," he advised, the fine fabric of his suit teasing lightly at her bare skin as he leaned forward to lay the dryer on the dressing table. "I know you often stay late at school on Wednesdays, and I just wanted to tell you not to tonight. We'll be going out—the two of us and Cynthia."

"Sorry, but I won't be able to make it," she warned him with acid regret. "You two can go without me."

"Not a chance, sweetheart." In a possessive gesture he took her by the shoulders, smiling when her startled gaze lifted to meet his in the glass. "We're going to present a united front—the three of us as a family."

"Well, I can't," she objected. "I've been gone for three days, and work will have been piling up on my desk. Professor Brandenson——"

"Will have made sure that there's plenty for you to do," John finished for her. "No doubt about that. The old despot seems to spend most of his time finding new ways to keep you busy."

"It's all part of my job! I'm supposed to——"

"What? Be a doormat? Let him walk all over you while you do most of his work?" John inquired sarcastically. "The man knows a good thing when he sees it, and you must be the best slave he's ever had. You've spent the last month jumping when he's told you to, not coming down until he's given his permission."

"It's a privilege to work for him," she explained, striving for a cool note—anything to avoid focusing on the way John was gripping her shoulders. "I'm honored that he trusts me enough to let me do some of his work. Well, I am," she insisted when she saw John's arch and skeptical expression. "You don't understand!"

"Of course not," he agreed mildly enough, but she knew she'd made a mistake when she saw how he stiffened and the proud lift of his head. "How could I? I'm the ignorant high-school dropout. I couldn't possibly understand the demands of higher learning."

"That's not what I meant," she countered, shocked that he should even think such a thing. She knew that he didn't love her, possibly didn't even like her very much, but surely he knew that she wasn't a snob? "You know that I don't——"

"Do I?" he asked softly. "In fact, I know almost nothing about you . . . except that I should assume that most of what you said last summer was a lie."

"And what about you?" she demanded, stung by the injustice of his accusation. "Do you expect me to believe that you never lied to me?"

"Perhaps neither of us was totally honest," he conceded with cool smile, "and perhaps we each got what we deserve . . . which doesn't change anything now. I want you home early tonight, Serena. End of discussion."

"It's not," she persisted stubbornly. "I can't tell Professor Brandenson I want to leave early tonight. If I do he'll tear me to shreds."

"Then don't tell him. Just leave," John suggested, a hint of steel behind his words. "Be home by seven."

"And if I'm not I suppose I'll be punished by you."

"No, not punished..." He ran his hands lightly across her shoulders, carefully fingering the fragile bone structure. His gaze and then, reluctantly, hers was drawn to the movement. Fascinated, she studied the contrast between his tanned and capable hands on her softer skin. "I'm not like the good professor. I don't browbeat people into submission."

"No?" she asked, using sarcasm as a defense against the insidious effects of his touch.

"No." His hands moved on, down her arms, a feather-light caress. "I use more inventive, more pleasant methods to get my way. If you're late I'll think of something," he promised, bending his head, the crisp vitality of his hair brushing her cheek when he touched his lips to the curve of her shoulder. "I'll see you at seven, sweetheart," he murmured. "Don't be late."

CHAPTER FOUR

BEFORE Serena could object again, John had released her; he was gone from the room before she could even turn to watch his departure. Not that he was really gone, she realized, brooding into the mirror. He didn't need to be physically present to dominate her thoughts. He'd left his mark on her that first day; by the time it had ended she'd been a different person, all her actions and reactions changed . . . because of him.

If that moment in the graveyard—when he had held her close to free her from the thorns—hadn't been enough to bind her to him he would have succeeded by the end of that first evening—that mystical, magic evening . . .

"This is fantastic!" Serena exclaimed when the business of ordering had been accomplished. She was probably being too enthusiastic; a man like John Bourque was undoubtedly more accustomed to taking out blasé sophisticates, the kind of women who would accept without comment this charmingly converted old mill.

Well, so be it! she decided with a defiant toss of her head. He already knew she wasn't a sophisticate, and she was suddenly feeling uncharacteristically daring. For once, she wasn't going to play it safe; she was going to be the person John made her feel she really was—intensely alive and unafraid to let her feelings show. "Three JN stones and dinner at a place like this," she marveled, her daring balking at the idea of adding John's name to the list of her good fortune. "I can't believe my luck today!"

"And I can't believe mine." He smiled at her over the rim of his glass, his gaze silently holding hers for a long time, before he changed the subject. "Tell me about JN," he directed, "and everything about old burial grounds."

"I don't know everything about old burial grounds, and no one knows much about JN," Serena admitted, then remembered what John had said about hiding her light under a bushel and forged ahead, "but right now I definitely know more about him than anybody else. He's considered to be among the technically best of the early carvers. His work is unmistakable, and he sometimes carved his initials on his stones, but no one knows his name. There's only his work to speak for him, and I've just found three of his stones that I'm sure aren't listed in any books. They're all fine examples of his work, and one in particular is very different, something he never tried anywhere else..."

She was off and running, blossoming under John's apparently rapt attention. She'd been asked to discuss a subject she knew well and loved, and through their meal she waxed eloquent, even expansive. It wasn't until the waiter was forced to interrupt to ask if they'd like coffee and dessert that she realized that John couldn't have got a word in if he'd tried.

"I've talked too much," she said, stricken, returning to earth with a resounding crash. "I've bored you to tears."

"I haven't been bored. I learned a great deal."

"Stuff you couldn't possibly want to know."

"Serena, I'm willing to learn anything," he assured her, a puzzling intensity behind his words. She heard it clearly, and he knew she had. "Look," he continued, suddenly serious, "I was fourteen when I dropped out of school and went to work—an extreme example of teenage rebellion and the burning drive to be independent."

Heavens! She didn't think she'd ever before met anyone who had dropped out of school, certainly had never known anyone who had had so little formal education—not that the lack was apparent, she acknowledged. "What did your parents think?" she asked, eyeing him with new curiosity and respect.

"They weren't around to express an opinion," he answered dryly. "My father...who knows?" he continued with a brief, dismissing gesture. "I never knew much about my father except that he walked out before I was old enough to have any memory of him. My mother died when I was twelve, and for the next two years I was what's euphemistically called 'a ward of the State'—in and out of a few foster homes."

"How awful!"

"No, not really awful," he told her with a second dismissing gesture. "Mostly pretty dull, living with people who were singularly lacking in imagination. By the time I got to high school I couldn't see any compelling reason not to go to work, so I skipped."

"And certainly made a success of yourself," she put in fiercely.

"In due course," he agreed—no false modesty for this man, she noted. "Unfortunately it left some terrible gaps in my education, and I can't think of a topic I wouldn't want to learn more about."

"But Puritan graveyards?" she demanded, skeptical laughter hiding the wealth of feeling she wasn't sure she could handle. "No one cares about Puritan graveyards!"

"You do."

"But I'm different."

"Yes, I'd noticed that," he acknowledged with a slanting smile, "but the question is: are you different enough? Do you mind spending the evening with an intellectual failure?"

Was he mad? she wondered, smothering a nervous laugh. She was the dull little bookworm; did he seriously think she minded anything about being with him? "Of course I don't mind!"

"No? You're well on your way to a doctorate, and I'm a high-school dropout."

"You don't seriously believe that?"

"It's the truth."

"But doesn't experience count for something?" she countered, staunchly partisan. "Look what you've accomplished—while I've been in school or grubbing around old burying grounds you're one of the people who's been changing the Boston skyline."

"Some people don't like the changes in the skyline. They'd say it proved my point."

"But I'm not one of them."

"You're not a snob? Serena Winslow Wright——" he spoke her name carefully, deliberately, spacing out the syllables "—is not a snob?"

"Certainly not," she snapped, thinking of Lillian. "I despise that sort of thing."

"You can afford to. Serena Winslow Wright—Winslow, as in Governor Winslow of Plymouth Colony, I suppose. You came on the *Mayflower*, didn't you?"

"Not personally. That was a bit before my time," she responded coolly, wishing—hoping—he wasn't serious. "And I'm not descended from Governor Winslow, but from his younger brother, Kenelm, and he didn't come on the *Mayflower*. He came several ships later, and he was nothing so grand as a governor. He was a carpenter."

"Several ships later," John repeated with a wry expression. "That makes him a real newcomer, doesn't it? Not 1620, but something a whole lot later—like 1623?"

"Something like that," she agreed, smothering a smile. "Listen, if you want to hear about *Mayflower* ancestors, I've got one for you. I've got John Billington in my family tree—or, more likely, dead drunk under it. He's not exactly an ancestor to be proud of—trouble from the start, and the first man hanged in Plymouth Colony. Is that classy enough for you?''

"Still, it's more——'' he began, then finally got her point. "Am I being unduly sensitive?"

"I think so," she answered diplomatically, "but I can't believe that it's typical of you."

"Not usually," he conceded with an approving— probably even grateful—smile. "It's just that I'd suddenly grasped the enormity of having dinner with Serena Winslow Wright."

"Don't you think I'd grasped the enormity of having dinner with John Bourque?" she shot back. "Some of the people I work with would give their eyeteeth to have dinner with you."

"Because of my money?"

"For some of them, yes. You'd definitely be worth cultivating because of the possibility that you might finance a research project. If you didn't have a dime, some women—even in dusty old American Studies— would kill to go out with someone who looks as good as you do... and there are some," she continued hastily because, for all her new-found courage, she didn't want to end on the note of his attraction, "and I include myself in this category, who would be impressed because you do important things. You do practical things, things that matter in the world, while we just sit around, contemplating our intellectual belly buttons."

"Oh, Serena!" He threw back his head and laughed. "You're not at all what I expected."

"And you're not what I expected, either."

"Then we're even, aren't we?"

She'd thought so then, completely unaware of the game he'd been playing with her. It hadn't occurred to her that who she was—her name—mattered in the least to him. And she certainly hadn't thought he was playing a game later, when he'd stopped the car in front of her house and hitched his arm across the back of her seat. "Am I going to see you again?" he'd asked directly.

She'd nodded, equally direct—too happy to play coy by pretending to give the matter careful thought. "Yes, I'd like that."

"Good. So would I." His fingers trailed lightly across her shoulders, slipped into her hair. For the second time that day, he removed the pins. "There, that's better," he said approvingly when her hair came tumbling down. "I like you wild."

Wild? The word echoed in her mind. He liked her wild—she who had never been wild, who didn't know how to be wild . . . although she was feeling just a little wild right now, she realized. He had found her nape and begun to caress it, his fingers moving with slow and rhythmic pressure. Delicious, she thought, closing her eyes as he continued—and she discovered just how erotic that small gesture was.

"Serena, may I kiss you?"

"I wish you would," she confessed, captivated by his touch, reveling in his nearness, tantalized by the musky and masculine scent of his body. Never before had she felt this kind of wanting, never felt so drawn to a man. She needed his kiss—how else could she feel whole? she wondered—but when his lips finally touched hers a new world of wanting opened to her.

A kiss—John's kiss—was only a place to start, she realized vaguely. Slow and gentle, almost careful just at first, he led her deeper and deeper into the mysteries of being close to a man. He coaxed her, teased at her senses until her lips finally parted beneath the warm pressure of his. His possession seared her to the core, ignited feelings and sensations she hadn't known she possessed. When he drew her even closer she went willingly, her body melting against the hard frame of his, her hands gripping his shoulders.

Have I done this to him? she wondered when she heard his ragged breathing match her own. She sensed his loss of control, marveling that his need could be as great as her own. I don't believe it! she exulted, her last conscious thought before she heard the words repeated some unknown time later.

"I don't believe it," John murmured, reading her mind, she was sure. They were that close now, she fiercely told herself, that attuned to one another. What other explanation could there be? "Absolute magic," he continued unsteadily, still holding her close, settling her head on his shoulder, his lips briefly touching her temple. "Lord, it's been years... Serena, sweet Serena... when can I see you again?"

"Any time. Whenever you like," she answered dreamily, trusting him completely...

Which was the worst mistake you ever made, she told her image in the mirror, finally leaving that first summer night behind to face the reality of the gray October morning. To have let him take over like that! she rued, and then stopped herself. Why are you doing this? she demanded of her reflection. Why are you wasting so much time, reliving the mistakes you made, the lies he told? It was pointless, and yet... it was funny how the past had suddenly started to repeat itself.

Last night, when he'd taken the pins from her hair, he had kindled her memory of that first time, and the second—memories she'd thought were so deeply buried that they could never hurt her again. And this morning, when he'd got in his cracks about Professor Brandenson, he had forcibly reminded her of that first evening, the only other time he'd let her see how he felt about his lack of education. The only difference, really, was in his presentation. What she had cherished as signs of the relationship developing between them had become sources of the conflict between them, new ways for him to wound her.

Worst of all, though, was the way he could still make her respond to his presence. Nothing, heaven help her, had changed about that! No matter how badly he had hurt her, no matter that she now knew the truth, when he touched her she still went up in flames, the past not so much repeating itself as rising up to slap her in the face.

Given the time she'd spent fighting with John and the bout of remembering which had followed, Serena knew she was going to be late for Professor Brandenson's Wednesday morning conference. She also knew that he considered an unblemished past record no defense against a first transgression, which meant that he was going to be furious with her. In fact, he was so angry that he interrupted himself, mid-monologue—an almost unheard-of occurrence—to tear into her as soon as she entered the meeting room.

"What are you doing here?" he demanded, his voice thundering over the heads of the others gathered around the large oval table. "This department sends you off to a conference—at great expense—and you don't even have the courtesy to arrive on time the next day! You force me to change my plans for this meeting, you deprive your colleagues of the opportunity to profit from what you ought to have learned at that conference... Inexcusable!"

For a man who looked like Santa Claus in tweeds, Serena reflected, tuning out as he continued to pile abuse on her, he had the killer instincts of Attila the Hun. Right now he was making absolute mincemeat of her, enjoying the first chance she'd given him, she supposed, taking the philosophical approach, then snapped to attention as one unexpected phrase penetrated her calm.

"No more than I expected when I learned that you had deceived me!"

Deceived him? How had she deceived him? Serena wondered, knowing better than to question this improbable avenging angel. Whatever the transgression, she'd know soon enough.

"When I agreed to have you as my assistant you were single," he accused. "I expected—and I made it clear that I did—that you would devote yourself totally to your work and mine. Had I known, had I had even the slightest suspicion that you were planning to marry someone—a fact which you most conveniently neglected to mention—I would never have taken you on. If you're going to let your work suffer while you play newlywed games...if you and your groom can't restrain yourselves during working hours...well..." He hesitated, perhaps sensing from Serena's outraged expression that he'd gone almost too far.

He was a great one for personal attacks, and Serena had sat through enough of them directed at others, but this time he'd far exceeded the bounds of good taste and fair play. Especially this time! she told herself. Given that there had never been any so-called newlywed games between herself and John, the professor's charge would have been funny if it hadn't been so unpleasant.

"Well," he said again, disconcerted by Serena's smoldering silence, "if you ever, ever again pull this kind of stunt, you'll be fired on the spot."

"That was so unfair!" Judy, Serena's closest friend in the department, came up to her after the meeting, pink-faced and indignant. "I couldn't believe he was so angry with you—not after you've worked so hard."

"Oh, well—it happens to all of us," Serena pointed out, finding it difficult to be too concerned. Of the two tyrants in her life—the professor and John—she found the professor's abuse infinitely less dangerous. "And I suppose it could have been worse."

"I don't see how," Judy said with a shiver, "and it was so wrong of him! You've got to be the best teaching assistant he's ever had. No one works harder than you do, no one stays later or does more of his work.''

"Maybe that's where I've gone wrong," Serena suggested, refusing to acknowledge that John's opinion of the professor might have influenced her thinking. "This is the first chance I've given him to dump on me. Maybe he's held that against me.''

"But he has no right to," Judy sputtered, "and he shouldn't have dragged in that bit about your marriage. That was disgusting!"

"Not in very good taste, anyway," Serena put in mildly, but Judy would have none of her forbearance.

"It was a lot worse that that, and he should have known better! It's the most unfair thing he said, too. Your husband must be some kind of saint—putting up with all the long hours and the work you take home.''

"He's no saint, believe me," Serena assured her unsteadily, suddenly fighting a case of the giggles. John a saint was worth a good laugh, although she supposed she ought to be taking more seriously Professor Brandenson's threat to fire her.

He was, after all, a towering figure in the rarefied world of American Studies, and to spend this year working for him would do wonders for her career... a career which suddenly didn't seem to matter as much as it had in the past. For years it had been the most important—the only!—thing in her life: a calm and predictable world, one in which her accomplishments mattered—not her name, or her family's social position. It had been a relief to escape from Lillian's and Cynthia's world of intrigue and gossip, where appearances always mattered more than substance.

School and—in due course—Serena's career had always been vitally important to her, had always come first... until she'd met John. In the summer, when she had thought they were in love, she had all but forgotten her work, fitting it in only when she couldn't be with him.

And now? What was happening now didn't make sense, she reflected as she worked her way through a long busy day. She was doing what had to be done, but she didn't seem to care—not even about Professor Brandenson's tirade and his threat to fire her. She knew she ought to be terrified of losing her job, but her life was being dominated by John's towering presence, making everything else seem insignificant.

Not that she still loved him! she hastened to assure herself. She despised him for what he had done to her, feared him for what else he might do. There was no love left, but he still was—as he had been in the summer—more important than work, more absorbing.

Well, you can't let him be! she lectured herself, and finally succeeded in exorcising him from her mind so she could tackle the tall stack of term papers Professor Brandenson had dumped on her desk with curt instructions to have them all graded before she left for the day. A huge job, she reflected grimly, but not impossible, and a good way to make up for the transgression of coming late to his meeting.

When she finally permitted herself a brief break she could see that she'd made definite progress. The uncorrected pile was noticeably smaller; with luck she'd get through all of them and avoid another of Professor Brandenson's outbursts. Back to work! she urged herself, stretching, checking the clock on the wall of her tiny office, pleased to see that it was only a bit after seven——

Seven! she thought, instantly on her feet. John expected her home by seven and she'd forgotten—forgotten or refused to remember, she allowed, not that it made any difference. Either way he was going to be furious with her, and Professor Brandenson's wrath was no longer important. John was the one to worry about.

He was in a dangerous mood, she reflected, racing home, in an absolute fever to get there as soon as possible. Things between them had changed—and not just because of Cynthia's sudden appearance, Serena thought. She should have known that there would be limits to John's willingness to let their relationship exist as a cool business arrangement. From the start it had been inevitable that some time he'd begin to force the issue and make demands on her. She'd had nearly a month of relative calm, nearly a month of John's forbearance, but now that had ended.

She was going to be—she glanced quickly at her watch—nearly an hour late, and she had no idea how he'd react. Would he think she'd deliberately disobeyed him? Would he be angry? Silly question! What frightened her wasn't the prospect of his anger, but how he would express it. What had he said? That there were pleasant ways to get her to do what he wanted—an idea that didn't bear thinking about. There was no telling what he might try; all Serena could do was brace herself for the confrontation.

What confrontation? she found herself wondering just a few minutes later. After her worrying it was something of a letdown to discover, almost as soon as she let herself into the house, that a confrontation with her was the last thing on John's mind.

"Oh, it's you!" Cynthia exclaimed, the first to notice Serena poised on the threshold between entry hall and living room. "We'd begun to think you weren't coming."

"I couldn't help it. I got held up," Serena announced, a thread of defiance directed at John—not that it mattered, she noted. John wasn't even looking at her.

Between them, he and Cynthia had a cozy thing going. The living room was dark, except for the warm glow and shifting shadows cast by the fire blazing on the hearth. The two of them were seated on the couch, two beautiful people, not touching—at least not at the moment,

Serena qualified—but they were very close, each half turned to face the other. All she could see of John was his back: broad shoulders and fine tailoring, but Cynthia's appearance spoke volumes. She was leaning toward John, giving him the best possible view of her undeniable charms. She was wearing a glittering little cocktail dress which left almost nothing to the imagination, her lips glistening, her hair in artful disarray.

As though she'd just been kissed, Serena realized, experiencing a swift stab of something like pain, hating herself for admitting to an emotion so irrational, so—so juvenile! She was behaving like a teenager, as though jealous of Cynthia for taking a new boyfriend away. If Serena had cared about John—which she didn't, she assured herself quickly—this would have been a bad moment. The details of this intimate scene spoke volumes, as did Cynthia's new dress and the fur jacket carelessly draped over the arm of the couch—both bought with John's money, Serena was willing to bet. Obviously, Cynthia was doing very well for herself, and she and John seemed to be enjoying each other's company.

So what? Serena asked herself. John was nothing to her, so what did she care? But she did—if only, she hastened to assure herself, because of feminine vanity. No woman liked to feel like an outsider, the one denied admittance to any charmed circle which contained an attractive man.

She was, she discovered, more human than she would have thought possible. It hurt to feel so... so left out, and John only made things worse when he finally turned to look in her direction. He was smiling—but not for her, Serena knew. He'd been smiling at Cynthia—amused and indulgent—and it took a moment for that smile to fade, to be replaced by a sharp and questioning stare.

"What happened—darling?" he asked, stressing that meaningless word, playing at being the loving husband—

although why he should bother, Serena thought indignantly, when she was almost positive that he'd just been
kissing Cynthia... "You said you'd be home by seven."

"Yes, but Professor Brandenson got angry with me,
and I had to stay after——"

"Honestly, Serena," Cynthia exclaimed on a bubble
of laughter, "you sound just like a schoolgirl again.
Made to stay in after—that's priceless."

"But she still is a schoolgirl, in a manner of speaking,"
John pointed out with a quick glance at Cynthia, "and
Professor Brandenson is serious business. His approval's
important to Serena. You're not in too much trouble, I
hope?"

And what do you care if I am? Serena wondered,
staring stonily at him for a moment, fighting the hard
glint in his eyes—a demand that she play the game too.
"No." Finally she capitulated—but only this once, she
promised herself. "I forgot the time. I stayed late to grade
papers for him."

"Did you get them all done?" John asked casually,
and she shrugged.

"Nearly. I can finish tonight, just so long as I get
them on his desk first thing in the morning..." She trailed
off, realizing that John didn't care about the details of
her work; what mattered to him was the fact that she
hadn't followed his orders. "I am sorry I'm late."

"No harm done. You've still got time to change," he
told her, consulting his watch. "Cynthia discovered that
pile of invitations we'd been ignoring. She went through
them and found one that appeals to her—some kind of
charity thing, a champagne reception. We can still make
it...if you don't take too long," he called after Serena
when she turned and started for the stairs, his words
sounding not at all like the command she knew they were.

One she did not intend to obey, she had decided by
the time she reached the first landing. They could go
without her. John had a nerve, thinking she would

mindlessly obey him—particularly now, when it was obvious what had been going on just before she'd walked in on the two of them!

Once in the bedroom she closed the door behind her, wishing again that she could lock it, then sank into the bentwood rocker. It was a relief to empty her mind, she discovered as she slowly rocked back and forth. She wouldn't think about John, or that cozy scene she'd interrupted.

"Serena?" She started at the sound of her name and looked up blankly, needing a moment to comprehend that John had silently joined her and was already closing the door behind him. "Are you all right?" he asked, sounding concerned—still playing the game, Serena noted, in spite of the fact that Cynthia couldn't possibly hear him. "You haven't even started to change."

"I'm not going," she announced baldly, meeting his dark and smoldering gaze. "You don't need me! You've got Cynthia, and the two of you looked to be having a very good time when I walked in just now."

"What's the matter, Serena?" he inquired pleasantly enough, inspecting the contents of her wardrobe, casually selecting a dress and laying it on the bed before coming to stand before her. "Don't tell me you're jealous."

"Of course I'm not jealous," she snapped—which was true, she hastened to assure herself. Her feelings were like jealousy, but somehow different...possibly some kind of territorial urge? she wondered. After all, John was her husband, even if their marriage was in name only, and she did have her pride! But jealous? "Under the circumstances, I'd hardly feel jealous."

"Or feeling a little left out?" he persisted, ignoring her denial, staring down at her for a moment before reaching out, his hands at her slender waist, drawing her to her feet. "You shouldn't—there's no reason to be," he told her, still holding her by the waist, his voice an intimate murmur, his breath stirring her hair. "I don't want Cynthia—there's no fun in taking what's offered so freely, but you're different, sweetheart. I like a challenge—and you're certainly that."

"I don't care—what you like—what I am," she stammered breathlessly, trying to twist out of his grasp, instead finding herself inexorably drawn even closer to him. "Please—let me go!"

"Not a chance..." he shook his head, smiling at her "...at least not until you agree to come with us tonight."

Come with the two of them—did he think she was crazy? "I won't," she insisted, and something within her finally snapped. "Maybe you're having fun, but I'm not, and I'm not going to waste an evening at some pointless party. You're the one who cares about Cynthia," she accused, "asking her to stay here, letting her run wild with your charge cards——"

"What's the problem?" he cut in with ominous calm. "Afraid there won't be enough left for you?"

"Of course not!"

"Or for Daddy? Is he falling a little behind with his bills?"

"Leave my father out of this," she warned, although why she should do anything to defend him wasn't quite clear. His behavior had been every bit as bad as John's, but it was John she was angry with now. "He has nothing to do with——"

"He has everything to do with this arrangement, and if you think——" John paused for an instant, his face an expressionless mask, only his blazing dark eyes giving a clue to his feelings "—if you think I'm going to renegotiate terms when I've got nothing to show for what I've already paid for——"

"You've got social standing. You've got Cynthia eating out of your hand. Isn't that enough for you?"

"Not at the moment," he said grimly. "Right now I expect you to change your clothes and be ready to leave——"

"I'm not going," she said again, stamping her foot.

"All right, if you insist..." Remarkably he smiled, but his grip on her waist was suddenly stronger, and Serena felt herself being drawn closer to him. "Since you won't go out, we'll stay here, and I'll take something else that I paid for."

"You wouldn't dare!"

"That's like waving a red flag to someone like me," he advised, still smiling. "Of course I dare. How do you think someone with no social standing got this far in life? I've always dared to take what I want."

"But not from me!" Serena tensed as he forced the first contact between her body and the long line of his. "I'll fight you."

"Not for long," he promised on a soft note of laughter.

But Serena knew that there was nothing funny about this. He was too close now, and already her resolve was beginning to weaken. Beneath his veneer of fine tailoring she was acutely aware of his hard-muscled strength and his masculine scent—a heady mix of plain soap, astringent after-shave and mellow wood smoke. She still despised him—of course she did!—but she was already melting, her will being consumed by the heat of his body.

Nothing but physical need, she tried telling herself, but the knowledge was no help in combating the desire and delicious excitement coursing through her. His lips had begun to seek hers, and it was just like the summer, she thought vaguely, like those long summer nights when she'd thought she could trust him, when she'd believed... So why, now that she knew... how could she let him win?

"Damn you," she spat, fighting his power, gathering the scattered remnants of her resolve in time to turn her head away from his kiss. "You win. I'll go with you."

"Yes, I thought you would, given sufficient inducement," he agreed evenly, releasing her so quickly that she nearly lost her balance—while his was intact, she noted bitterly. "Hurry up and get changed," he directed after a brief glance at his watch, "and don't even think of telling me I can't stay here while you do."

"What is it?" she demanded. "Do you get your thrills by watching?"

"If I wanted thrills, sweetheart, we wouldn't be going out," he told her, laughing when he saw her outraged expression.

CHAPTER FIVE

SERENA heard herself being hailed by a girl about her own age, someone else wearing what obviously was the uniform for this kind of party: artfully disordered hair and clever little cocktail dress. "Serena! I don't believe it!" The girl approached, scattering exclamatory statements as she continued her chatter. "Renie, you're actually here...the first time anyone's seen you since the wedding...it's been ages...we'd begun to think the two of you had just disappeared and were never going to be social!" She finally managed to make it through the crowd. "It must have been some honeymoon," she finished, eyeing Serena expectantly.

Just like the others: wanting to hear all the private details, Serena thought, buying time by dredging a shrimp through the cocktail sauce, popping it into her mouth. It was years since she'd been to one of these parties, but nothing seemed to have changed—except her own status. She was one of the young marrieds now, married in fact to the hot topic of conversation. Everyone wanted to be her oldest and dearest friend, the better to get a juicy titbit from her to pass on to everyone else.

"It's been busy," she offered briefly, going for another shrimp. These were Cynthia's friends, Serena reflected. She had no idea who most of them were, although they all seemed to have been at the wedding—Lillian would have seen to that; she'd made sure all the right people had received invitations. Still, Serena didn't remember this girl, though she'd used Serena's nickname. "Renie" went back to her childhood, suggesting that they'd known each other years before. Perhaps they'd attended the same nursery school; for a while they might even have been good friends.

But that had been so long ago! How, Serena asked herself, was she supposed to know who everyone was? She'd spent most of her adult life deliberately avoiding this kind of social whirl—and with good reason if tonight was an accurate example. She knew that there was more to Boston society than this; there were people from the best old families who lived quietly and worked hard and almost never came to parties like this. Not everyone cared about glitter and gossip and being seen at all the best social functions, but there were plenty who did.

Most of them were the wives of very proper men, Serena realized, noting on this girl's ring finger the plain gold band and family diamond in its antiquated setting. The husbands were lawyers with Boston's very proper firms, or officers of Boston's very proper banks; they lunched at their very proper clubs, supported very proper charities. They were busy and important men, but their wives led pretty empty lives—or would have, had they not devoted themselves to the pursuit of what was clever, fashionable, and the "in" thing. These were the people Serena had always tried to avoid—women who, she realized now, were a lot like Lillian and Cynthia. Their superficial chatter had always made Serena uncomfortable—Can't they talk about something interesting? she'd often wondered. Now she was positively hating the way they tried to ferret out the most intimate details—as the girl who had hailed her was doing now, hoping for something specific about Serena's sex life with John.

"Come on, Renie," the blonde coaxed now. "What have the two of you been doing, hiding away for the whole month since your wedding?"

"We haven't really been hiding," she protested, then slipped into the deliberately vague response she had well-rehearsed by now. "The trouble is that we both have pretty busy schedules. John's work is very demanding, and I'm still in school. That doesn't leave us much time to party.''

''But plenty of time to stay in, I bet,'' the blonde observed with a wicked grin. ''If I were married to a man like that I don't think I'd ever get out of bed.''

Did the girl seriously think that kind of leading would work? Serena wondered, taking refuge in another shrimp, and killing two birds with one stone, she reflected. It wasn't until they'd arrived at the party that she'd realized how hungry she was, that she'd been too busy all day to remember to eat. The shrimps, she'd discovered, were delicious, with the added attraction that they gave her time to decide how to parry each thrust. ''Mmm, well...I suppose...'' she finally responded. ''I mean, there are things that have to get done, aren't there? Responsibilities.''

''How dreary!'' The other girl laughed, dismissively tossing her head. ''Personally, I'd say to hell with responsibilities if I were married to someone like that. He's gorgeous!''

He was that, Serena acknowledged, instinctively seeking John's tall presence, following his progress over the rim of her fluted champagne glass. In fact he was incredibly handsome—a dashing figure—in his well-tailored, very proper evening clothes. When he smiled, as he did now—strong white teeth contrasting with what remained of his summer tan—Serena felt her breath catch, and forced herself to look away.

''We've all been wondering about him,'' the girl confided, her voice dropping to a gossipy between-you-and-me murmur, ''what he is—ethnically speaking,'' she explained when she saw Serena's blank expression. ''You know—is he Greek, or Italian, or Spanish...? We've been trying to figure it out. I mean, he's so dark, and so sexy looking...he must be something exotic, but we don't know his background, do we? Except you, of course. I'm betting he's got gypsy blood.''

''Is this some kind of pool?'' Serena inquired with acid sweetness, seething inside. The nerve of these people—making a game of something like this, talking about John behind his back! ''Whoever gets it right wins?''

''Oh, not quite like that!'' The girl shrieked with laughter. ''But we're all dying to know...Renie, tell me! Am I right? Is he a gypsy?''

''Well, actually...'' Serena leaned closer, taking malicious delight in leading the other girl on—striking a blow for John, she supposed. No matter what he'd done to her, he didn't deserve to be the butt of this empty-headed blonde's speculation and jokes! ''Actually, he's...an American.''

''An American?'' the blonde asked blankly, then an impatient expression flickered across her features. ''Oh, Renie, I know that! But what was he before?''

''Who knows?'' Serena shrugged. ''And does it matter? Like all of us, if you go back far enough, he came from somewhere else.''

''Well, I didn't!'' The girl stiffened, now very much on her dignity. ''I don't see how you can say that. My family's always been here!''

''But it can't have been,'' Serena persisted, enjoying every minute of this, ''unless you're all American Indians.''

''We're certainly not,'' the blonde snapped—clearly, American Indians were too ethnic for her. ''You know what I mean!''

''But only American Indians can say that they've always been here,'' Serena pointed out, ''although even that's not strictly true. They came from somewhere else, too. They've just been here longer—at least ten thousand years longer—and they must have had a harder time getting here than anyone else. Walking across the Bering

Straits during the last Ice Age must have been rough—
even more of an accomplishment than coming on the
Mayflower."

"Do you mean...?" The other girl hesitated, dig-
esting what Serena had said. "I get it," she began again,
pleased with herself and—finally—with Serena. "You're
telling me that he's an Indian!"

"No, I'm simply saying that, if tracing your ancestry
back to an early arrival is what makes for social clout,
then the best clubs would be full of Indians, they'd be
on the boards of all the best charities, and there would
be a lot of them at this party. Don't you see?" she
finished in her best lecturing tone. "The whole thing
about background doesn't mean anything."

"Very clever," the blonde said coldly. "You always
did go on about all that stuff you read in books, making
the rest of us feel as if we were dummies. Honestly,
Renie, you haven't changed."

"But none of us does—that's the point." Serena
smiled, abandoned the shrimp and moved on. She'd just
lost herself one so-called old friend, she reflected, wondering if this girl had connections John had hoped to
cultivate. Well, just too bad for him if he did! He thought
he'd been clever, marrying her for her social position,
but he should have checked her out a little more
thoroughly. If he had he'd have learned that she didn't
give a tinker's damn about that kind of thing, that she
was as likely to alienate the "right" people as to attract
them. Poor John! she thought maliciously; he'd paid all
the money for someone who would be no help at all.

Unless he felt he didn't need her help, she speculated,
deftly acquiring two puff-pastry canapés as a waiter
passed with a tray. Perhaps just her name and her family
background—which had got them invited to this party—
were enough. There was no denying that, once here, he
seemed to be doing very well on his own. He was re-
lating to people with just the right mixture of deference

and self-confidence, nothing of the crude social climber about him.

It was nicely done, she conceded, and just as nicely done was his expert job of charming Cynthia, who seemed always to be near him. His idea or hers? Serena wondered, watching as he bent his head to say something obviously very private to her. Cynthia responded with a merry peal of laughter and John smiled indulgently as the two of them moved to join a new group of people.

They had a lot in common, Serena brooded, wishing she had the strength of character to look away. Unlike her, they both clearly loved this kind of party, both knew how to fit in perfectly. I'm the odd one out, she acknowledged; I'm the one who thinks this kind of evening is deadly dull. They were having a grand time while all she wanted to do was get home and tackle the last of the term papers waiting for her in her briefcase.

It was nearly midnight before she got the chance, and it meant leaving John and Cynthia together in the living room, drinking brandy in front of the fire. It was enough to make her feel like Cinderella, Serena thought, enjoying the absurdity of the idea as she slowly climbed the stairs, briefcase in hand. To be fair, she conceded, John had asked her to join them, and she'd taken perverse pleasure in refusing. Stay with the two of them while they rehashed the party? No thanks! she assured herself as she closed the door to her study, shutting out the murmur of voices from below.

Two hours later she was finished—not her best job of grading, she had to admit, but at least they were done. All that was left to do was to get to school early enough to beat Professor Brandenson to his desk. She'd have done what he wanted—which ought to help her earn back his approval, she told herself, carefully tucking the term papers back into her briefcase and leaving the study. On the landing she paused, realizing that nothing had changed while she'd been buried in her work—from the low murmur of voices she could tell that John and Cynthia were still downstairs.

Finding a lot to say to each other, Serena thought waspishly—not that she was jealous! In fact, the more time the two of them spent together, the better it was for her; John couldn't harass her while Cynthia kept him occupied—thank goodness for small blessings, Serena told herself. Quickly she changed into a nightgown, turned off the bedroom lights and climbed into the four-poster bed.

She lay there, staring into the darkness, determined to stay awake until John finally came up to bed—not because she cared how much time he spent with Cynthia, Serena assured herself, but as a precaution. She wouldn't put it past him to try to take advantage of her if he found her asleep in his bed, and she wanted to have her wits about her when he finally entered the room!

What finally awakened Serena was the sensation, even with her eyes closed, that the room was filled with sunlight. That was odd, she thought sleepily, burrowing into the pillow. There wasn't supposed to be sunlight. It was nighttime, some time between two and three in the morning; she was waiting for John—wasn't she? Of course she was! Waiting for him, and for the inevitable clash there would be when he finally left Cynthia and came up the last flight of stairs.

Still, it was awfully bright for three in the morning, she mused, and cautiously opened her eyes. It was sunlight, she saw instantly. It was morning, and she couldn't prevent a rueful smile. Last night's busy thoughts, her clever plan to defend her outraged virtue—all for nothing. It had been silly of her to worry when John had so obviously been occupied with Cynthia... Fully occupied? Serena wondered briefly before her thoughts skittered away, unwilling to examine that issue.

Turning, about to get up, she saw the note on the pillow next to hers—a cream sheet of paper on the cream linen, the black ink an emphatic contrast. Just like John, she thought with a shiver, pushing herself into a sitting position, picking the note up by the edges.

I decided to let you sleep and turned off your alarm. Don't worry about the term papers—I'll drop them off on my way to work. I'll also fix it so you won't need to go in today, and you and C. will meet me for lunch—Dante's, at one.

As ever—John

"As ever—John"—what was that supposed to mean? Serena brooded, staring down at the uncompromising black ink, the characters just as uncompromising—all harsh angles and slashes. His handwriting told her all she needed to know about him: his impatience, his drive, his decisiveness, his conviction that people would do what he told them to do.

In those few words he had taken charge of her day— or thought he had, she told herself, crumpling the sheet of paper, throwing it across the room. The nerve of him! It was time that he learned that he couldn't get away with that kind of high-handed behavior! she decided, her temper flaring. She was going to university today, no matter how he thought he'd fixed it so she wouldn't have to, and she certainly wasn't going to meet him for lunch. Instead, she decided, her resolve fueled by her growing anger, she would take the battle to him now, make it clear—once and for all—that she wasn't going to let him run her life!

In spite of the attention lavished on her hair, her clothes and her makeup, she reached the offices of Bourque Properties and Construction in less than an hour. She'd been there only once before, and only briefly, but that had been during the summer. Back then she'd fancied herself so in love with John—fool that she'd been!—that she'd had eyes only for him, and had paid no attention to her surroundings.

Now, stepping off the elevator into the large reception area, Serena could see just how designed to impress everything was. Rich dark wood paneling on the walls, deep-pile silver carpeting underfoot, a circle of comfortable chairs upholstered in a medium blue fabric, a couple of choice antique pieces—all in the best possible taste, she had to admit. She'd expected to see several good paintings, but realized instantly why the walls were bare. The offices were high up in one of the towers John had built, and he—or, more likely, his decorator, Serena told herself spitefully—had been wise enough to see that even the best art couldn't compete with the view from the floor-to-ceiling windows: a breathtaking sweep of the harbor and its small islands. Today the sky was a deep, vivid blue; the water a darker shade, with cresting waves providing the occasional white counterpoint; the islands a mixture of green and the soft crimson and gold of turning leaves. There were colors no artist would dare try to capture, she decided, so absorbed and soothed by the scene that she briefly forgot why she was here.

"May I help you?"

The well-modulated voice barely penetrated Serena's spell, but she turned to focus on the attractive receptionist guarding the double doors to John's private office.

"It's Mrs. Bourque, isn't it?" the receptionist prompted expectantly.

"Yes." Well, that made it easier, she reflected, attempting to marshal both her thoughts and her anger. At least she wouldn't have to suffer the indignity of having to prove that she really was John's wife, with a perfect right to be here to interrupt him. "I'd like to see my husband, Now, please."

"But he's not here," the receptionist told her, sounding mildly regretful. "He's at the site."

"I see..." She should have called, Serena realized, some of her new-kindled anger directed at herself for having wasted time on this wild-goose chase. "Which site is that?"

"The new tower."

"And where is that?" Serena persisted.

"On Broad street." Now the receptionist sounded surprised and slightly doubtful. She probably can't believe that I don't know where the site is, Serena fumed, feeling that she'd been put on the defensive. "It's not far, but I'm not sure...you may not be able to see him."

"I'll see him," Serena assured her with grim determination, turning on her heel, punching the button to summon the elevator.

It wasn't her fault that she didn't know every blessed detail of what he did with his time! It wasn't her fault that they didn't sit around every evening, discussing their work. With that devil's bargain he'd made with her father John had shut her out of his life—and forced her to shut him out of hers, Serena told herself, feeling cheated. For an instant, alone in the elevator, pain mixed with her anger as she considered what she and John could have had together—what he had once suggested they would have...

"Are you afraid of heights?" he'd asked one summer day, and when she'd said she wasn't he'd smiled. "Good. Some day we'll go to the top of one of my towers."

"Why?" she'd teased. "To show me what you do, pay me back for all the time I've made you spend in graveyards?"

"It's not a question of paying you back," he'd told her, unexpectedly serious. "I've enjoyed our time in graveyards. I like watching you at work, when you're so absorbed that the rest of the world doesn't exist for you..."

"Do I neglect you?" she'd asked quickly with a pang of conscience. "Do I make you feel left out?"

"Of course not. My ego's not that fragile," he'd assured her, laughing, "but we can both be pretty intense about our work, and I thought, perhaps if you know something of what I do, we'd have that much more in common. Besides, I think you'll like it up there. It's a heady feeling...something elemental and very free about being at the top of a tall building before the roof and windows shut out the world. You'll see," he'd promised, smiling.

Well, now she was about to see, but this visit was nothing to do with having things in common, Serena told herself, her steps slowing as she saw ahead, on the side of a building, a sign with John's familiar logo. It was simple enough, clean and uncluttered, a stylized rendering of the Boston skyline and one word, "BOURQUE," in uncompromising black capitals.

The building carrying the sign appeared finished, at least at eye level, but it was still cordoned off. Uncertainly, Serena stepped in front of the stepped-back entrance, wondering how to gain access. There was no sign of John—had she really expected him to be standing on the pavement? she asked herself, wondering what she should do. There were plenty of workers around, men and—to her surprise—a few women, mostly in casual, sometimes even grimy work clothes and hard hats. They all seemed busy, their actions intimidatingly purposeful, and she hesitated to bother any of them.

But she knew she had to do something. She'd been furious when she'd set out to find John, but her anger was pretty well gone, and now even her courage was deserting her. If she stood here—wavering on the pavement—much longer, she'd turn tail and run, leaving nothing settled between them. So do something! she urged herself, and in that moment heard someone calling her name.

"Mrs. Bourque? Over here." One of the workmen had created an opening in the barricade; he stood by it, beckoning to her. "I guessed it might be you," he told her when she was closer. "The boss told me to be on the lookout, that you'd be coming today."

John knew, damn him! Instantly realizing what he had done, Serena felt her anger rekindling. The wording in the note had been deliberate, chosen to offend her because he knew how she would react. He'd set a trap for her, and she'd been fool enough to walk into it. It was almost enough, she seethed, to make her leave, except that leaving would deprive her of the pleasure of telling him off. She needed that now, needed the satisfaction of wiping that smug and knowing expression off his face.

She thanked the workman—after all, John's behavior wasn't his fault, she reminded herself—and forced a polite smile. "I don't want to be a bother. Could you just tell me where to find him?"

"Up there." The workman gestured vaguely, leading her inside the building into a vast unfinished cavern of concrete. "Here, you'll need this," He stopped by a rough storage box, producing a hard hat.

"That?" Serena asked, disbelieving when he handed it to her. "You're not serious?"

"Afraid so." He grinned apologetically. "I hate to make you mess up your hair—if you're anything like my wife that's the one thing you can't stand—but no one's allowed on the site without one."

"I feel like an impostor," she confided while he waited, polite but inflexible, for her to cautiously settle the hard hat on her head. "I thought only the people working had to wear these."

"Nope. Everyone does," he assured her, leading the way toward a large steel-mesh cage. "This is a dangerous place if you don't take precautions. You wouldn't want someone dropping a wrench on your head from ten storys up, would you?" he asked—silly question, Serena thought, repressing a nervous laugh—then hailed a man standing inside the cage. "Pete, you've got the boss's wife for a passenger this time. I'll let him know she's on the way up.''

The cage proved to be a elevator, but its ride was like no other elevator ride Serena had ever taken. As the cage moved slowly upward she could look out through the wire mesh as they passed floor after unfinished floor of dim and echoing space. Then, as the almost ponderous ascent continued, the world beyond the cage grew lighter. They passed floors where the windows had yet to be installed, then floors which were lacking exterior walls, until they finally emerged into the open. Obviously, they had reached the top of the building; there was nothing but blue sky all around them. No walls, Serena saw, no ceiling, no floor above this one, no roof; nothing but blue sky...and John, waiting for her just outside the cage.

There was something about him, she realized instantly. It was more than the sight of him, the stark white hard hat he was wearing a curious contrast to his usual well-tailored suit. There was something...elemental, she decided, about the way he stood silhouetted against the bright October sky. This was an alien world—windswept and severe, filled with the harsh sounds of construction—but it was his world, one he had caused to exist...the one he commanded.

So that was why he'd made sure she would come here—to put her at a disadvantage, she saw, her temper gathering steam again. He wanted her on his home ground, where he was in control and she would be out of place. Well, it's not going to work! she vowed. She didn't care how high they were, didn't care how close she came to the edge—or the possibility of a drop of who knew how many feet. Right now she was too angry with him to be frightened; she proved her point by stalking past him into the no-man's land of construction and high altitude. Instantly the wind attacked, so fiercely that she instinctively grabbed for her hard hat.

"Careful, sweetheart," she heard John say above the wind as he caught her by the waist, effectively holding her in place. "The winds are strong up here."

"Don't!" She pulled away from him, bracing herself against the buffeting of the wind. "Keep your hands off me!"

"But I wouldn't want you to be blown over the edge."

"I'm already over the edge," she snapped, ignoring the activity around them, the curious glances of the workers. "You drove me over the edge!"

"Did I?" he inquired silkily, watching her with a speculative half smile. "I can't imagine how."

"By meddling..." she paused to rummage through her bag until she found his crumpled note, the one she'd thrown across the room and then retrieved as she was leaving, determined to preserve it as ammunition "...with this," she continued, holding it aloft. "With what you said in this, and what you had the nerve to do this morning——"

"What? You call that meddling?" Casually he draped one arm over her shoulders, drawing her away from the confusion of activity around them, heading toward a space relatively free of workers and equipment. "All I did was drop those term papers off on my way to work. There was no reason for you to get up at the crack of dawn to see that they made it to Brandenson's desk before he did."

"And what about fixing it—fixing it!—so that I wouldn't have to go in today?" she demanded, forced to pull away from him again. "You don't call that meddling?"

"I caught the great god's secretary on her way in, explained that you had a lousy cold... That's meddling?"

"You know it is!"

"Well, perhaps a bit," he had the grace to admit, "but at least I didn't beard the lion in his den and play the outraged Victorian husband, give him hell for making you work twelve and sixteen-hour days—which is what I bet you thought I'd done.''

It was, of course; she hadn't worked out the details, but she'd been sure he'd taken on Professor Brandenson and said such terrible things that she might never be able to undo the damage. ''But still,'' she persisted, refusing to be mollified, ''you had no right——''

''I think I did.'' He moved away from her, going to stand closer to the edge of the building than she would have liked, nothing but a single strand—rope, she thought, or possibly steel cable—between him and the terrible void. ''I am your husband, after all.''

''In name only,'' she reminded him, forced to raise her voice above the wind.

''True.'' He stood, hands deep into his pants pockets, rocking slowly back and forth, staring down into the depths beyond the edge. ''But I think that counts for something. You did marry me, when you could have called it off.''

''What choice did I have?'' she demanded, balking at the thought of getting any closer to the edge, forced to stare at his unrevealing back and strain to catch his words. ''If I'd called things off my father would have been ruined.''

''It wouldn't have been as bad as that,'' John offered, a cool business assessment. ''Without the money I put up a lot of people would have known how bad his losses were. It would have taken him a while to dig himself out of the hole. He'd have been publicly embarrassed, but ruined? No, unless being publicly embarrassed counts as ruin in your world.''

''It's not my world,'' she countered, and John turned his head to look at her, just long enough for her to see his skeptical expression. ''I know you don't believe me, but it's true—I got away from it years ago! If I hadn't had to marry you I could have stayed away.''

"Back to square one," he observed dryly, still rocking back and forth against a panoramic view, a crazy quilt of rooftops and a few other taller buildings. "This argument is going around in circles."

"All our arguments do that," she noted bitterly. "It's a fundamental problem, when——" She broke off, eyeing his tall form. He was making her feel definitely queasy, she realized. She knew he wasn't really as close to the edge as he seemed, but she didn't like the way he appeared to keep leaning into the abyss, never pulling back soon enough for her peace of mind. "Will you please stop?" she demanded sharply. "You make me nervous."

"I don't see why. Wouldn't it solve all your problems if I fell off? You'd be the rich Widow Bourque—all that money, without the inconvenience of a husband."

"That's not funny!"

"No?" he asked ironically, and then, turning his head again, he saw her face. "Sorry," he said more gently, relenting, stepping back a pace. "I didn't mean to frighten you, but it was enlightening. I think you must care—at least a little more than you're prepared to admit."

"Don't——" She stopped dead, staring at him. He was right, of course. She did care to a certain extent— a hold-over from the summer's high emotion...*her* high emotion, she amended quickly. There had been no high emotion for him, just cool calculation and the games of strategy he knew how to play so well. He didn't care, and she was damned if she'd let him see her weakness. "Don't flatter yourself. It's just that I don't like heights as much as I thought I did—not like this," she told him briskly. "How far up are we, anyway?"

"Thirty-two storys."

"With no walls and no glass... It's a little too real for me."

"Then we don't need to stay," he offered, instantly obliging, shooting a quick glance at his watch. "We could go to lunch now, if you like."

Lunch! She'd completely forgotten lunch, the other bone she had to pick with him. "I'm not going to have lunch with you and Cynthia," she announced, brandishing the crumpled note. "You can't order me around!"

"Another argument?" he asked with exaggerated patience. "This soon?"

"Yes, this soon!" Did he think he could get away with a condescending attitude? "I don't need to waste my time having lunch with you and Cynthia just to be part of some grand design of yours. If you want to have lunch with her—fine! Go ahead, but don't think you can drag me along!"

"But I've got to drag you along," he said patiently, as though talking to a child. "I don't want people to begin speculating, wondering if there's something going on behind your back. Sorry, Serena, but the last thing I'd do is let myself be seen alone with Cynthia."

"Hypocrite," she accused. "You worry about appearances, then spend all kinds of time alone with her—like last night—when there's no one around."

"You were around last night."

"That's not the same thing, and you know it! Besides, I was working, and then asleep. The two of you had a clear field...you could have been doing anything."

"Doing anything," he repeated thoughtfully, but there was a dangerous glint in his eye. "Now there's a euphemism that covers a multitude of sins, any number of which you seem to think Cynthia and I committed."

"I don't think anything of the sort," she countered hotly, skirting the truth. "I don't waste my time thinking about you and Cynthia, and I certainly don't care what the two of you do together. What I hate is the pretense, all this business of trying to make things look good. I hate it!''

"And yet you do it so well," he observed, a dangerous glint in his eyes. "You carried it off last summer, well enough to win Daddy the prize, and now—well, you may protest, but only in private, I notice. In public you've done your best to maintain appearances. Balk now and you could ruin everything."

"You're threatening me!"

"When I have to—yes," he admitted cheerfully, "but you know you've got to do it anyway. It's part of the bargain."

"And I have no choice," she murmured wearily, all her anger gone, replaced by a black cloud of depression. Fighting him was hopeless. He was better at it than she was; he always played to win, and the bottom line was that he held all the cards. As long as she stayed married to him she would have to accept the fact that he was in control. She had no choice at all.

"All right," she said finally, opening her hand to release his crumpled note. So much for ammunition, she thought, watching as the wind took the note. For a moment the cream paper danced between them, sailing higher, before a down draught caught it and it disappeared over the edge of John's tower.

CHAPTER SIX

AFTER the first few sips of her Bloody Mary, Cynthia began to come alive, abandoning her morose silence for a little flirtatious grumbling. "Honestly, John, you're unfair!" She paused for dramatic effect, daintily nibbling on her celery stalk. "It's nice of you to offer lunch, but not when I have to get up so early to make it."

"Little girl, you're bone lazy," he teased, then remembered to offer Serena a conspiratorial smile—more pretense, she thought, his smile leaving her cold—before he turned back to Cynthia. "One o'clock's not that early."

"But we stayed up so late," she protested prettily. "I could have slept hours longer, and I don't even know why we're here."

"To have lunch, of course."

"There's no 'of course' about it," she contradicted, eyes narrowed to study his face. "With you, there's always a hidden agenda, something you hope to accomplish... Honestly, Renie, I don't know how you stand him!"

"Neither do I," Serena murmured, ignoring the warning glint in his eyes. "It's like living with a chess champion. He's always three moves ahead, while I try to figure out what's going on."

"Exactly!" Cynthia nodded emphatically, then turned back to John. "So what's the move this time? Why are we here?"

"The truth?" John asked Cynthia, but it was Serena who answered.

"For a change—why not, John?" She kept her tone light, but she could see that it wasn't enough to please him. A muscle knotted along the clean line of his jaw as he cast her a dark look.

"We're here," he finally said very deliberately, as though talking to two very slow children, Serena thought indignantly, "because Josiah Stuart often has lunch here."

"Gregory's father?" Cynthia demanded disgustedly. "Are you going to expect me to be charming to him?"

"Yes," John answered firmly, making it clear that he wasn't giving her any choice in the matter, "if he comes."

"And if he doesn't?" Cynthia persisted, refusing to take John seriously—a mistake, in Serena's opinion. "May I behave badly, be generally disgusting and rude?"

"No. Some of his friends are here, and sure to mention that they saw you and your sister having lunch with me. We want things to appear very normal—and very proper."

"Oh, yes, proper," Cynthia agreed on a sour note. "And dull."

"Your reputation could stand some dullness," John pointed out dryly. "Whether you know it or not, you're skating on pretty thin ice—give his father any excuse——"

"And he'll make sure that Gregory cuts me adrift," Cynthia completed, a bitter edge to her voice. "Yes, I know. I've always been on thin ice with Gregory's father—it comes of having such dubious parentage."

"That's ridiculous," Serena interjected. "You shouldn't think that."

"Why not? Gregory's father does," Cynthia countered. "I'm only a Wright by adoption, and legalities really aren't good enough for the Stuarts. Daddy may think of me as his daughter, but there's no telling who my real father was—someone common, no doubt.

"You see, John?" she continued, turning back to him. "That's how it is for those of us who weren't born into the charmed circle—we can never be completely respectable. It doesn't count for much that Dad married Mummy—it was that dark secret first husband who fathered me, and the Stuarts will never forget it. I'll never be good enough for Gregory."

"That's not what Gregory thinks," Serena put in, staunchly partisan, but Cynthia merely shrugged.

"Perhaps," she conceded grudgingly. "I know that wasn't what he thought when we were dating. Then he was so crazy about me that he didn't care about any of this old family stuff. His father knew that he couldn't stop us—we were going to get married, with or without his approval. Besides, Mr. S couldn't say no without insulting Daddy—that's one good thing to have come out of being a Wright by adoption."

"One good thing," John repeated with emphasis. "Then you'll concede that there's something good about staying married to Gregory?"

"I'm not sure I'd go that far," Cynthia objected, but her smile gave John points for debating. "It was fun at first, fun for a while..."

"Then give yourself some time to decide what you really want," he urged. "Don't hand the Stuarts an excuse to kick you out of the family. They've always been above common gossip, and they won't make an exception for you. If you want to keep your options open you'd better behave."

"Behave," Cynthia repeated, sounding pained. "I hate that word. People have been throwing that word in my face for years, and I'm sick of it... Sick of behaving, too. It's such a bore, and just once——"

"Just once—this time—you'd better think before you do something outrageous," John told her, and for the first time there was impatience in his voice. "The last thing you need is to create a family scandal."

"You do go on about family scandal," Cynthia observed, her expression growing harder, her eyes beginning to glitter—the way they always did when she was about to say something completely outrageous, Serena knew. "This business about not tarnishing the old family name and all that...but the joke's on you, John. It's not as though the old family name had never been tarnished before—not that you would have known about it, of course.

"You see, almost no one knows," she continued, enjoying the knowledge that she had John's undivided attention—Serena's, too, because she had absolutely no idea what this dark secret was, what Cynthia knew that she didn't. "A lot of people have their suspicions, but no one can prove a thing...and it's not the kind of thing anyone would ever tell you. You're an outsider, and no one would dream of telling an outsider any of our dirty little secrets. The old families stick together."

"I'm aware of that," John allowed dryly, "but we're both outsiders, so why not tell me?"

"I wonder...should I?" Cynthia mused, eyeing him thoughtfully. "If I do you won't be pleased. You see, you paid top dollar for the family name, but what you bought was damaged goods—no, don't blame your wife," she told him when she saw his dark gaze quickly shift from her face to Serena's. "It's not her fault. It's Daddy's dirty little secret...and I think that's how it ought to stay," she decided abruptly, "but you don't need to worry about saving the family from its first scandal ever. There's already been one—a whopper, bigger than what there would be if I decided to divorce Gregory."

Then, to Serena's amazement, Cynthia dropped the subject completely and slipped back into her polished routine of social chatter—as though nothing had happened.

*   *   *

"At lunch, what was that all about—what you wouldn't tell John?" Serena began when she and Cynthia were finally back in the house on Birch Court. After lunch it had been Cynthia's idea to do some shopping, and after several hours of hectic activity and constant interruptions Serena finally saw her chance to clear up a mystery. "I don't know about any family scandal."

"Oh, that," Cynthia said absently, busy sorting through the accumulation of boxes and bags, checking each purchase to separate Serena's few from her own. "That was nothing," she explained vaguely as she finished the job. "I made it up."

"Made it up," Serena repeated blankly. "Why would you do that?"

"To get back at John." Cynthia aimed a toe at her own stack of dress boxes, pushed them out of the way and went into the living room. "I'd had enough of his lecture, and I thought—well, why not rattle his cage just a bit? So, I made it up—couldn't you tell?"

"No," Serena said bluntly. "You made it sound very real."

"Oh, well..." Cynthia drifted toward the drinks cabinet, sorted through the decanters, then poured herself a stiff measure of Scotch. "I've always been good at that sort of thing. It's the only way to survive when no one wants you to have any fun—not that it's working with John. He's worse than Mummy and Dad ever thought of being—behave, Cynthia...keep your options open...you're on thin ice," she mimicked. "He's driving me nuts!"

"But it's for your own good," Serena cautiously suggested. "He's only trying to help you."

"To help himself—that's more like it," Cynthia said shortly. "Can't you see what he's doing? It's not enough for him that he bought into this family. Now he's after Gregory's father. Josiah Stuart has ten times Daddy's clout and he could be incredibly useful to someone like John."

"Oh, I don't think that's why," Serena began doubtfully, and Cynthia cut her off with a brittle laugh.

"Of course you don't. You're so naive about things like this—you couldn't even see why John was marrying you, so it's no wonder that you can't see what he's doing now. Do you want some?" she asked in a quick switch, reaching for the decanter again.

"I suppose so," Serena decided, hating herself for taking the bait, but the temptation was just too great. She was dying to hear more, so she accepted the drink Cynthia poured for her, settling in one of the wing chairs by the empty fireplace. "How can you be sure you know what John's doing now?"

"Because I'm just like him," Cynthia explained with a complacent smile, taking the other wing chair. "We're two of a kind, and I know how his mind works. He's always after the main chance—he has to be! No one ever helps an outsider, and that's what we are—we're always outside, looking in, wanting in . . . and when it's like that you use any edge you can get," she finished, knocking back more of her Scotch in one swallow than Serena would have dared attempt.

"But you and Gregory?" Serena persisted. "Can keeping the two of you together really help John?"

"Of course. Otherwise he wouldn't bother," Cynthia said with a careless shrug; then, when she caught Serena's puzzled expression, she laughed. "Poor Renie, that's something else you don't understand about people like us. We're really unprincipled. We don't care about other people, not in the bleeding heart way someone like you does. We take care of ourselves—which is why John's prepared to sacrifice me."

"Sacrifice you?"

"Mmm." Briefly, Cynthia's brow tightened into a frown. "He knows I don't want to go back to Gregory, that it would be better for me if I didn't, but the Stuarts matter more than I do. When John talks about avoiding a family scandal he's not worrying about our family. He doesn't want any mud to stick to the Stuarts, and when he pulls it off—if I let him pull it off, and I probably will—he'll make sure Gregory's father knows who to thank...

"Don't you see, Renie?" she asked, noticing Serena's blank expression. "Josiah Stuart can do so much for John—and I'm not talking about business, because they already do business together, at least on occasion. No, we're talking about the intangibles..." She paused long enough to get up and pour herself another drink. "Little things, like the occasional lunch at the Somerset Club, membership at the Country Club in Brookline... There are lots of things Mr. S can do for someone like John, given a reason to be suitably grateful...

"And there are lots of things John can do for me if I give him a reason to be suitably grateful—if I'm a good girl, if I behave myself and go back to Gregory," she continued after a moment. "Mr. S isn't giving us that much to live on these days, and I could do with more spending money, new clothes, some good jewelry... all of which John could do for me—which is how these things work, Renie."

"It sounds pretty cold-blooded," Serena observed distastefully, "and not very nice."

"Oh, well, I never said it was nice, but cold-blooded?" Cynthia smiled—a secretive, satisfied little cat's smile, Serena thought. "I don't think you could call it cold-blooded."

"No?" Serena asked sharply. "When you'd go back to Gregory just for what it would get you?"

"Why not? I married Gregory for what it would get me," Cynthia pointed out. "John married you for what it would get him—does that make him cold-blooded? When he makes love to you can you honestly say he's cold-blooded? Oh, you don't need to answer that," she said, laughing, when she saw Serena's stricken expression, "but you know what I mean."

But she didn't, Serena admitted, trying to ignore the unexpected stirring of discontent. She could imagine—she wasn't as innocent as she'd been before she met John, not even as innocent as she'd been just a few days ago—but she didn't know...and probably never would. "I think—it's a terrible way for things to be," she finally managed, and Cynthia laughed again.

"You would," she jeered, "but you're stuck with it, just the same. We all are—you, me, John...even Gregory, I suppose. Heaven knows, I don't want to go back to Gregory, and—all things considered—I think John would be happier if Gregory and I broke up. I know he'd rather not have me go back to Houston," she added, preening, running one slender hand through her artful blond curls. "We—well——" she paused, the satisfied little cat's smile back again "—we wouldn't mind being able to see each other from time to time...if you know what I mean."

"Are you warning me?" Serena asked, surprised that her voice sounded so even. "Or is this a threat?"

"Neither one," Cynthia told her, getting up to pour herself a third drink, bringing the decanter back with her, adding more to Serena's glass. "I'm just being realistic about this whole business. After all, we're both adults now and there's no sense pretending...

"Look," Cynthia leaned forward, confiding, "this isn't a competition. It's inevitable, Renie. John's that kind of man, not the type to stay faithful long. He's incredibly attractive, very sure of himself, a man who has power and knows how to use it. A man like that always has—well, strong appetites...and, to be realistic, you are not the world's most experienced girl. You can't know very much—except what he's taught you—which means that it won't be too long before he gets bored.

"Maybe he already is," she decided after a moment's thought. "You must have noticed that since I got here he's been paying a lot of attention to me. You know as well as I do that he finds me attractive, but there's more to it than that. He and I can play the same game, know what we're getting into, know how far we want to let things go..."

"And it's pretty obvious that you'd like to let things go all the way," Serena remarked—her turn to be bitter, although she wasn't sure why. Hadn't she decided, within the last twenty-four hours, that it would be better for her if something developed between John and Cynthia? Intellectually, she still knew she was right, but something was happening to her emotions. What was safe and sensible was suddenly in conflict with what she wanted...and what she wanted was for John to want her! "And I'm not supposed to mind—is that right?" she demanded, her tone more revealing than she would have liked. "I'm supposed to ignore what goes on between the two of you, just pretend that it doesn't exist and wait for you to go back to Houston."

"That's the general idea," Cynthia agreed casually, "but cheer up, Renie. It's really not all that bad. At least you know that I'm not going to break up your marriage. You've got real power—you've got the family connections. John knows that being married to you gives him respectability and a place in society. He'll always be very discreet about his affairs, and he'll never divorce you— which is a lot more than most wives can be sure of.

"So what's the harm?" Cynthia finished, the whole thing settled—to her satisfaction, Serena noted resentfully. "When I go back to Houston he'll come back to you. You have nothing to worry about! If you love him as much as you did last summer—and I'm pretty sure you do—you won't mind his occasional fling."

*   *   *

Cynthia was right. In the late afternoon Serena curled up in John's bed and contemplated the truth. "If you love him as much as you did last summer—and I'm pretty sure you do..." She did. In spite of what he'd done to her, she hadn't stopped loving John. For the last month, since their wedding day had blown up in her face, she'd been sleepwalking through life: not thinking about him, not letting herself feel anything for him. All the time, though, the feelings had still been there, just waiting for something to reawaken them.

In the end it hadn't taken much to accomplish the task. Cynthia had arrived, forcing Serena into closer contact with John...proximity, a slight shading of jealousy...and in less than two days her numb little world had been destroyed. All of last summer's feelings were back—raw nerve endings which responded instantly to John's presence, proving that she still loved him.

So—what now? she asked herself as light gradually faded from the sky and shadows grew deeper in the room at the top of the house. She knew she had a real problem: how to protect herself from the pain of loving John. Her pride was a part of it; she could imagine no humiliation worse than letting him see how she felt. She had to find a way to distance herself from the power of his attraction, a way to preserve some part of herself for herself. At the same time she had to find some way to endure the inevitable pain of loving a man who didn't love her. At the moment the idea of John's and Cynthia's having an affair dominated her thoughts, but Serena knew that there were a thousand ways he could hurt her.

When you loved someone you were incredibly—devastatingly—vulnerable, she understood now. Anything had the power to wound—a thought, a fragment of memory, the sound of his footsteps on the stairs... coming closer, she realized, frozen in place in the center of the four-poster bed.

The door opened, and John's large shadow filled the doorway for an instant before he switched on a light. "Sorry," he offered when he saw her put a hand up to shield her eyes from the glare. "Would you rather I turned it off?"

"No!" She wanted anything but the intimacy of a shadowy bedroom, so she forced herself to accept the bright light. "It's all right."

"Yes, I thought it would be," he agreed, sounding amused, watching her while he shrugged out of his suit jacket and loosened his tie. "Did Cynthia remember to tell you that we're going out again this evening?"

"No," Serena told him, her voice cool and detached, "but I don't suppose that makes any difference. I'm just your puppet—when you pull the strings I have to dance, so——" she paused while she sat up and swung her legs over the side of the bed, instinctively checking to be sure that her robe hadn't pulled open "—when should I start to get ready?"

"Soon," he told her, ignoring her barb. "You went shopping?" he asked when he saw her few purchases, still in their gay boxes. "May I look?"

"Why not? You paid for them."

This time he shot her a quick, quelling glance, then opened the first box to inspect the maroon silk cocktail dress, its simplicity broken only by the row of tiny silk-covered buttons which marched from the neckline to the dropped waist. "That ought to be a good color for you," he decided, "although a little too proper for my taste——"

"I didn't buy it with your taste in mind."

"Of course not," he agreed dryly, investigating the next box. "Ah, but these..." Gently, he lifted out a satin and lace camisole and half slip in a slightly softer shade of maroon.

"Those were Cynthia's idea," Serena said quickly. "I wouldn't have…" She trailed off when she saw his quick knowing smile.

"Delicious," he murmured appreciatively. "Cynthia seems to have our best interests at heart."

"It's the sort of thing she buys for herself," Serena explained defensively, wishing she'd thought to hide them away—where he'd never find them!

"I'm glad she convinced you to do the same." He put the two drifts of fabric by the dress, fingered the lace for a moment, then laid them all on the bed. "Wear them tonight," he commanded, turning away. "I'll shower now, and give you a chance to get dressed— without having me as an appreciative audience," he called over his shoulder, closing the dressing-room door behind him.

Serena was off the bed like a shot, hurrying to be done while she had privacy. She made it, if only barely, and when he returned she was seated at the dressing table, putting the finishing touches to her makeup. Briefly, she ignored his presence while she applied mascara with a steady hand—a sign that she was calm and composed, she assured herself just before she looked in his direction. When she did she felt her poise beginning to crumble.

At the moment he wasn't even looking at her. Wearing only his trousers and a white dress shirt, his dark hair still damp from his shower, he was working on his shirt cuff links—head bent, absorbed by the task. It all seemed so… normal, she marveled, struck by the commonplace intimacy of the moment. They looked like any couple, savoring the last few moments of quiet before going out for the evening—an impression confirmed when he glanced up and found her watching him.

He smiled briefly, spent a moment inspecting her appearance, then nodded. "Very nice," he approved. Then he bent his head back to his cuff links, asking casually,

"What was Cynthia talking about at lunch today—that business about a family scandal?"

"Nothing. She made it up."

"Did she?" He finished with his cuff links and came to stand behind her, using her mirror while he worked on his tie. "Now why would she do a thing like that?"

"I——" She stopped, not wanting to be confronted by the Pandora's box of all the things Cynthia had said in that conversation. "How should I know?" she asked quickly—too quickly, she realized when, in the mirror, she saw his skeptical gaze. "She said—I don't know— something about wanting to irritate you. It was just a game."

"A strange kind of game," he observed, finishing with his tie. "So there is no family scandal?"

"Not that I know of," she answered coolly. Then she added, when she saw a new question forming, "Do we have to keep talking about it?"

"No, not if the subject bothers you." He reached out to touch her hair, watching the movement of his fingers as they began to toy with her curls. "Still, it's strange, don't you think? What family doesn't have at least one scandal hidden somewhere?"

"I don't know. I'm not familiar with that many families." She leaned forward, freeing her hair, then got to her feet, needing to put some distance between them. "You said we'd be going out soon," she reminded him from the other side of the room. "Shouldn't we be leaving?"

"Soon," he promised, studying her appearance. "You've lost weight."

"No. It's just the style," she explained self-consciously. She knew that the dress did hang too loosely, but no dress could emphasize what she didn't have; no one would ever say that her curves were abundant... unlike Cynthia's, she thought unhappily. Cynthia looked spectacular in anything. "I don't like looking as though I've been poured into a dress."

"You're too much of a lady to let yourself be poured into a dress," he told her, his smile taking the curse off the comment, letting her know that it wasn't just another of his barbs. "But this... needs something," he decided after a second brief inspection. "That gold chain. Do you know where it is?"

"No. You find it," she snapped, turning away to the window, brooding out into the darkness. She'd destroyed the slightly more comfortable current which had been running between them for the last few minutes— but only because he'd caught her off guard when he'd mentioned the chain.

Only a few days before the wedding they'd seen it in a shop window—an extravagant, glittering piece of jewelry, with large and elaborate gold links. "How do you feel about bondage?" John had teased, determined to buy it for her "for the fun of putting it on you some day." And then, inside the shop, when she'd tried it around her neck, he'd shaken his head. "You're too slight to carry it off—at least as a necklace. Try it as a belt." When she had, and it had fitted, there had been no doubt in his mind. "We'll take it," he'd said, and then, when the clerk's back was turned, he'd given Serena such an outrageously leering look that she'd dissolved into a fit of the giggles—so happy, so much in love... or so she'd thought.

"Here it is," she heard John say, then he was behind her, turning her to face him again. Without expression, he passed the chain around her, worked to settle it against the dropped waist of her dress, then fastened the clasp. "There—that's going to be better," he decided, his long, clever fingers making minute adjustments to the folds of her dress. "Much better... but you're still too thin," he told her, his fingers tracing her slender waist and the slight curve of her hips. "You're living too much on nerve."

"That's your fault," she accused, but there was a breathless, unsteady note in her voice. "Don't blame me!"

"I'm not blaming anyone," he reproved gently, drawing her closer, "but you could make things so much easier for yourself...and for me. Just relax, sweetheart," he coaxed, his lips touching her temple. "There's no need to burn."

"I'm not burning..." But she was. It took almost nothing to kindle the flame—no more than his clean male scent and his nearness, the heat of his body...his touch. What he did to her in moments like that made her greedy, forced her to acknowledge that she wanted more. He was so clever, she admitted, swaying toward him, and he made it seem——

"So easy," he murmured, his words completing her thought. "It's so easy—it could be so easy...just let yourself go."

"And let you take what you want?" she demanded, bitterness stiffening her resolve enough for her to pull away. "I'm not that big a fool!"

"Not yet, anyway," he allowed with the hint of a smile.

Not angry, she noted, merely amused—and supremely self-confident. Of course! He always was that, she thought, and the knowledge gave her the strength to regain her composure. "Can we leave now?" she asked crossly, and he nodded.

"Of course—but you're only postponing the inevitable."

He had the last word—damn him, she thought, and the worst of it was that he was probably right.

CHAPTER SEVEN

IT HADN'T taken Serena long to realize that tonight's party was almost exactly like the previous night's. It was just as dull, and populated by people who were just like those who had been at last night's party. Either that, Serena decided, or these were the same people—and all infinitely forgettable. There were the same stultifyingly proper husbands and the same bored wives—all of them wearing the same kind of clever—and skimpy—little cocktail dresses and the same artfully tumbled curls. All of them looked remarkably like Cynthia—the "Cynthia clones" Serena christened them—and a depressing number of them were thoroughly unpleasant, the worst kind of snobs.

"I think your husband's deliciously sexy," one of the clones confided to her. "I'd known for ages that he was attractive—one did see him around, after all—but I'd never spoken to him until a few minutes ago."

"Oh?" Serena smiled her now habitual noncommittal smile, then couldn't resist a gentle dig. "Why not?"

"Well, one didn't—you know," the clone offered with careless amusement. "None of us had met him, except some of the husbands—and that was business..."

"Which doesn't count?"

"Of course not! My dear, if we had to meet everyone our husbands do business with...well, think how many simply dreadful people we'd end up knowing!"

"In other words, people like John," Serena supplied with a sarcasm the clone missed completely.

"Exactly, although John doesn't seem terribly dreadful—I suppose he can't be or you wouldn't have

111

married him—and now that I've met him I don't think
it matters...I mean, it's rather fun, isn't it, to spend
time with a man who looks at you that way?"

"What way?"

"You know—you must know! It's that...little smile
you can see in his eyes, as though he's——" she paused
for a delicious shiver "—undressing you, thinking the
most outrageous thoughts."

"Perhaps he is," Serena suggested, wishing she could
believe that the little smile in John's eyes was because
he could see the hypocrisy of a woman like this.

"Oh, I don't think so," the clone concluded after a
moment's consideration. "Not yet, anyway. After all,
the two of you haven't been married long...surely even
he would know better than to start looking at other
women so soon? But when he does...well, you mustn't
be jealous," she advised with a laugh. "I don't think
there's a woman alive who can resist that kind of man...

"And the amazing thing is that he fits in so well,"
the clone continued enthusiastically. "Who would have
thought? It's not as though he was born with any advantages. He must have had to learn all this—how to
behave and do the proper thing."

"But it's not so awfully hard," Serena pointed out,
deciding that she'd had enough. It was time to put this
person—this creature!—in her place. "To be proper, all
someone has to do is be polite, remember a few basic
rules and then consider what to say—and what to leave
unsaid." She paused until she was sure the clone had
caught her meaning. "Of course," she resumed sweetly,
"some people spend a lifetime at it, and still don't get
it right."

The clone had the grace to blush—not a total fool,
Serena noted as she moved off, gratified to know that
she'd made her point.

"Serena!" Someone hailed her—another clone, leaning close enough to speak privately. "Poor Cynthia! She's having a rotten time, isn't she?"

"Oh, I don't know," Serena hedged, spotting Cynthia some distance away. She was standing alone at the moment, and Serena watched as a young man—a reasonably attractive one, too—approached her. He spoke briefly—something reasonably risqué by the look of his smile—and then, to Serena's surprise, Cynthia shook her head, deliberately moving away from him.

Behaving—doing what John had asked her to do, Serena could tell. Cynthia was finally following the game plan she'd outlined earlier. Her behavior would please him; in exchange he'd be suitably grateful. At the moment, though, Serena could see that Cynthia was paying what for her was a high price. Tonight—as a definite first—Cynthia wasn't the absolute belle of the party. Instead, she was playing Serena's old role of wallflower, and Serena enjoyed the irony—until she remembered what Cynthia knew: that John would reward her when the time was right.

"Do you see?" the Cynthia clone demanded, breaking into Serena's thoughts. "She's having no fun at all!"

"I think she's missing Gregory," Serena suggested diplomatically, scrupulously following John's strategy. That ought to please him—if he happened to be listening, she added in a mental proviso. Of course, he probably wasn't—a thought which inflicted on her an irrational sense of disappointment—because charming these dreadful people appeared to be demanding his full attention. "We thought it would be fun," she explained brightly, "now that we're both old married women, to have her come and visit, but I think we should have waited until Gregory could come with her."

"Be real, Serena," the clone advised wisely. "Your little sister's nose is badly out of joint. She likes to be the center of attention, but she's last year's news. You and your gorgeous husband are the novelty tonight, and Cynthia can't stand it. Perhaps I should try to cheer her—no, your John's taken her in hand, I see," the clone observed, discreetly craning her neck. "Isn't that nice," she asked rhetorically, watching for Serena's reaction. When there was none she made a small face—disappointed that she couldn't dig up any dirt—and began drifting away, spitefully adding, "Such a charming man."

Too charming, Serena told herself, wishing there were some of last evening's shrimps at this party. She wasn't hungry, but the shrimps would have given her something to do with her hands; as it was she had nothing to keep her occupied. For this evening's party, the planning committee had gone for a Japanese theme—sushi and saki, both of which Serena had been avoiding like the plague. She should have avoided the entire party like the plague, she told herself, hunting for a quiet corner and a brief respite from the manic gaiety.

She found it in a shadowy window alcove, an ideally isolated spot from which to watch the party...to watch her husband, Serena acknowledged honestly. He had finally noticed that Cynthia was alone and had taken pity on her. He'd joined her, instantly employing his patented charm to get her laughing. As Serena watched he leaned toward her, obviously to make a very private remark. When Cynthia laughed again, he smiled indulgently, drawing her arm through his.

They looked as though they belonged together, Serena brooded unhappily, remembering what Cynthia had said. She was right, too. They did have a lot in common. They actually liked this kind of party...and liked each other even more, although Serena doubted that they were in love. There was too much expediency in their relationship to leave room for being in love, but making love was a different matter. They'd find room for that—if they hadn't already... Would it happen tonight? Serena asked herself, afraid—as she watched them and noted the intimate smiles and meaningful looks they were exchanging—that she already knew the answer.

"Serena, darling! Don't tell me you're hiding."

"No, not really." She turned, pasting on a brilliant smile—someone to talk to, someone to drive her dark thoughts away. "Hello." Another Cynthia clone, although this one was vaguely familiar, someone she'd been at school with years ago—Serena was pretty sure of that... Daisy, or was it Maisie?

"I can't imagine what you're doing off in a corner," Daisy—if it was Daisy—told her, helping herself to some saki as a waiter went by. "If I'd married that devastating man I'd be sticking to him like glue."

"Devastating?" Serena repeated thoughtfully. "Well, yes, that's a good description of John." Involuntarily her gaze went to the small group of people dominated by her husband's tall, dark presence, Cynthia staring worshipfully up at him. "In fact, I can't think of a better one. John's good at devastating people."

"He's the hit of the party." Briefly, Daisy was silent, sipping her saki as she watched John's performance. "He's certainly got your sister eating out of his hand, hasn't he? But don't worry, darling, he's not likely to be indiscreet quite this soon—not when he owes his success to you."

"Even without me he'd have been the hit of the party," Serena told her, neatly sidestepping the loaded issue of Cynthia. "A devastating man is always a hit."

"Darling, he wouldn't even have been invited if it hadn't been for you," Daisy pointed out with exaggerated patience. "He's been tolerated at the larger charity functions—people wanted him to contribute, after all, but money can take a man just so far. He'd never have made the invitation list for something like this if he hadn't married you. I bet he still can't believe his luck."

"Any more than I can," Serena confided, laughing when she saw Daisy's puzzled expression. "Darling, it works both ways," she explained with her own attempt at exaggerated patience. "He got me, but I got him—a devastating man, instead of some dried-up, inbred brahmin."

"Well, yes, you got him. The question is, can you keep him?" Daisy raised her cup, then discovered it was empty. "Damn, I'm out of saki," she said with a little laugh, "and you don't have any...and I wanted us to drink a toast to—to luck," she decided.

"No, thanks. I don't like——"

"Don't be stuffy! We've got to drink a toast, and— heaven knows—you're going to need luck!" She hailed a passing waiter, appropriating two cups of saki, handing one to Serena before raising hers. "To you, you clever girl, for landing yourself such wonderfully virile new blood. Just remember—he'll need lots of care and attention, or he'll begin to stray."

If he hadn't already, Serena mentally added as they drank their toast, wondering if her bitterness showed. Wondering, too, what Daisy would think if she learned that Serena didn't yet know how virile John was—at least not directly...unless she counted that damnable night of the fourth of July...

"Confidentially, my dear," Daisy dropped her voice to a dramatic whisper, "I never expected someone like you to marry a man like that. I mean, you must admit, you were just the tiniest bit—well, different."

"Stuffy," Serena supplied cheerfully. "A book-worm...probably the dullest girl in the world."

"Well, you said it, darling. Don't blame me."

"No, I won't," Serena promised, forcing a laugh, asking herself why she bothered. Daisy knew. She was enough of a realist to have seen through the pretense of marriage to John. Of course Daisy knew—and how many of the others here tonight? Most of them, Serena grimly concluded. They were probably all laughing at her or—even worse—pitying her, but she could do something about that. She could do nothing to change the terms of this marriage, but she could make it clear that she wasn't the fool everyone—including John!—thought she was. Why not? she decided on a defiant note, drawing a deep breath and taking the plunge.

"Of course, it's really not that kind of a marriage," she confided, instantly assailed by second thoughts. What was she doing? she asked herself, staring down into her cup, wondering if the saki had been a mistake. She couldn't possibly have got drunk this quickly—could she? Surely not? And yet she felt out of control, compelled to show Daisy that she didn't care! "I know that—normally—John wouldn't look at me twice," she allowed, forcing yet another bright smile. "If it hadn't been for——"

"Hello, sweetheart. I've been missing you."

"Well, speak of the devil," Serena said, a hard edge to her voice, as John materialized at her side—just in time, too, she noted uneasily. She didn't know how, but he knew she'd been about to tell Daisy the truth. From across the room he had guessed Serena's intent and come to stop her—only something that important would have dragged him away from Cynthia! Now he was all easy charm, but his eyes were glittering dangerously, warning Serena that she could go just so far and no further. But two could play that game, she decided with sudden daring, and perhaps he wouldn't take her quite so much for granted when he realized that she held at least one weapon to use against him.

"This is such a coincidence," she said now, favoring him with a brilliant false smile. "We were just talking about you, Daisy and I. This is Daisy. I think we were in school together years ago," she explained carelessly, then took a deep breath and finished off her saki—for whatever additional courage it might provide. "She was just saying that I'm clever to have landed you—that is how you put it, isn't it, Daisy, dear? Of course," she continued, giving Daisy no chance to respond, "she doesn't really know what she's talking about—I don't think that she's figured out yet that I didn't do any landing."

"You're too modest," he told her, sounding indulgent, his hand on her shoulder. He turned her to face him, and only she knew just how strong was his grasp, what warning its pressure conveyed. "You should know by now—I was hooked from the moment I saw you."

"Were you really?" She met his gaze for a long pause, her own challenging his, daring him to make a scene. Finally, deliberately, ignoring his touch, she turned back to Daisy. "Now, I ask you, do you believe that someone this devastating—Daisy thinks you're devastating," she explained, turning back to John again. "Devastating and wonderfully virile. But really, Daisy——" it was time to turn back to her yet again, enough to make a girl dizzy, Serena thought, a sign that the saki was working "—do you really believe that kind of man—and John definitely is that kind of man—could get hooked on...on someone like me?"

"It was love at first sight." He reached for her, his hands spanning her waist, turning her toward him before she could pull away. "I knew in an instant that I wanted you."

"Wanted," she repeated, focusing on that one word, refusing to permit him to wound her with his easy lie about love. "Of course you wanted me, John, but that's not the question. The question is—why?" She reached up to brush an imaginary bit of lint from his shoulder— retaliation, in some small measure, for the way his long, clever fingers were toying with the gold links of her belt. "Most people already know, but there are a few still trying to figure it out," she told him, laughing up into his stormy dark eyes. "They're the naive ones, who aren't sure why you wanted me."

"Isn't that obvious?" He drew her closer, bending his head, his cool lips touching her cheek. "Sweetheart," he said for her alone, his breath stirring her hair, "you've gone far enough."

"I'll go as far as I like," she countered, fighting the sudden breathlessness that being close to him always brought on. "You can't make me stop!"

"Can't I? Just watch me," he promised in the same intimate murmur, then raised his voice just enough. "Sweetheart, I think the saki's gone to your head."

"That's not true!" She glared up at him, her stormy gaze clashing with his. "If you hadn't been paying so much attention——"

"To everyone else," he finished smoothly, then kissed her, effectively preventing her from saying anything else. "Poor girl," he added, amused, when he was done, "will you forgive me?"

"Never," she told him, which was true enough—how could she ever forgive him for all the ways he'd found to hurt her?—but it was difficult to maintain her anger, difficult even to think when his lips were teasing at hers. She'd been mad to believe she could challenge him when he was such an expert at fighting back...so clever, she thought with a sigh. He didn't care that they were in a room full of people, most of them probably avidly watching this scene. "Will you stop?" she whispered unsteadily, all her strength draining away as he continued his clever torment. "I can't think..."

"Good." His lips moved on to find an incredibly sensitive spot by her ear. "Don't even try."

She'd been a fool, she admitted helplessly, to let him destroy all her inhibitions... Already, she was melting against him, her body responding, burning at each point of contact with his. "Damn you," she finally managed, gathering the scattered remnants of her anger. "Let me go."

"If I do you might fall down."

"That's not true," she snapped, but he gave her no chance to pull away and prove her point. Oh, he was enjoying every minute of this, she fumed, embarrassing her before all these strangers, amusing himself at her expense... "Go to hell," she spat and he laughed aloud.

"Sorry, sweetheart, but I'm not going to oblige you. Instead, I think I'd better get you home... before you say things you'll regret."

"Things *you'll* regret," she corrected crossly.

"That too," he agreed, but only absently. He knew he'd won; they both did. She wasn't going to give away his secret this time, and already he was maneuvering the two of them through the crowd, pausing only long enough to collect Cynthia.

Thanks to the bracing night air, Serena's head was considerably clearer by the time she got into the car— not that it mattered, she noted, inwardly fuming. Cynthia was determined to reclaim John's undivided attention, delivering a litany of complaints—"... incredibly dull party... no fun at all... none of my friends there..."— and pausing only for John's soothing, sympathetic responses.

Just listen to him, Serena thought spitefully, her bitterness destroying the last effects of the saki. When had John ever shown her a scrap of sympathy? At the party he'd paid her almost no attention, none at all until he'd realized that she was about to be indiscreet. But Cynthia was a different matter; he didn't care if she was indiscreet and he could be indiscreet with her... and now, just because she'd had a lousy time at the party, he was doing his best to console her—although what he could do now was nothing to what he'd undoubtedly do later, when the two of them were alone... when they've got rid of me, Serena told herself, the thought fueling her anger.

Still, she didn't disgrace herself, didn't let them see her anger—or the irrational hurt which lay beneath. At the house she shrugged off John's attempts to help her out of the car. "Thanks, but I can manage for myself," she told him—very cool, very self-possessed, waiting silently while he unlocked the door.

Once inside, she headed straight for the stairs, and she didn't look back. She didn't want to see John and Cynthia, the two of them watching until she was out of sight. Obviously, they had plans for the rest of the night, but that didn't mean that she had to like the idea! What woman would? she asked herself, finally gaining the bedroom, not bothering to turn on a light. It hurt; it had to hurt! No woman liked to think that her husband was being unfaithful, and Serena was fast discovering that she was just as human as anyone else.

Knowing that John was being unfaithful—and with Cynthia, of all people!—really was some kind of cosmic joke, but Serena was past seeing the humor. It wasn't hurt she was feeling; it was an excess of raw emotion, hard to identify. Of course she cared that the two of them were going to make love; they had wounded her pride, come perilously close to destroying it!

Beginning to work on the clasp of the gold-link belt, she discovered that she was so angry that her fingers were shaking. Tonight she was the woman scorned, she thought, furious with John and Cynthia for casting her in the role, even more furious with herself for caring! Finally, she released the clasp and heard the chain hit the floor with a satisfying clatter. "So much for bondage," she said, her voice shaking nearly as much as her fingers, then set to work on the long line of buttons on the front of her dress. She hadn't even finished with the first one when something warned her that she was no longer alone; she looked up from her task to find that John had entered the room and silently closed the door behind him. Still dressed in the uncompromising black and white of his evening clothes, he was leaning against the door, watching her intently.

Briefly, her fingers faltered. "What are you doing here?" she demanded.

"I came up to see if you were all right," he told her, his face expressionless, giving nothing away.

Not that he cared, she reminded herself. His unexpected appearance was nothing more than—what? A guilty conscience? Or did he just want to make sure that she was tucked in for the night before he and Cynthia proceeded with their plans? Whichever it was, she refused to let it matter to her, refused to let him see her pain. With unconscious grace, she drew herself up to stand proudly, even defiantly, meeting his dark gaze while her fingers resumed their task, determined to prove that his presence had not upset her. "Of course I'm all right," she told him, trying for a cool note. "You can go back downstairs now."

"I hadn't intended to."

There was something about his voice, a thread of amusement, that was too much to take. After an evening of neglect and subtle abuse her cool self-possession snapped. "What about Cynthia?" she inquired sarcastically, forced to pause when she discovered that her fingers still weren't quite as steady as she would have liked. To work the first button free took all her attention, the second one nearly as much. "Won't she be disappointed," she finally resumed, "if you don't go back to her?"

"Perhaps," he acknowledged, shrugging out of his suit jacket, carelessly tossing it toward the rocking chair, "but Cynthia's feelings don't concern me."

"Well they have—this whole evening," she reminded him, managing the third button a little more quickly as her fingers acquired more skill. "You shouldn't start neglecting her now."

"Is that what this is all about?" he asked mildly, removing his tie, tossing it after his jacket. "Don't tell me you're jealous again."

"I'm not jealous! Just tired of watching the world—and you—revolve around Cynthia. Perhaps I was mistaken," she continued with elaborate politeness, continuing her work on the buttons, "but I'd assumed that we were supposed to—to look like..."

When she faltered, he favored her with a cynical smile. "A happily married couple," he supplied. "That's the general idea, not that you did much to promote it this evening."

"Not that I——" His accusation took her breath away. "You can say that when you spent the evening flirting with Cynthia—smiling and laughing, always right beside her? It was disgusting! Everyone noticed——" which probably wasn't strictly true, Serena admitted, but anger and humiliation had driven her beyond scrupulous honesty "—and they were all talking about it, all——"

"All your wonderfully social friends?" John broke in, a sudden hard edge in his voice, a dangerous glint in his eyes. "All those dear friends you grew up with, were at school with... the ones who think I'm not quite nice enough, that you married beneath yourself?"

She shook her head—did he seriously think that any of those people were her dear friends? Didn't he know? "It's not like that!"

"Of course it's like that! I know what they think of me—and say to you! Which is why, I suppose," he added reflectively, his brief show of anger gone as quickly as it had come, "you were about to let drop the terms of our marriage. Is that how it is in your social circle—marrying down is acceptable as long as there's enough money involved?"

"I have no idea," Serena retorted, the buttons forgotten as she seized a new barb. "Is it acceptable in your social circle to ignore your wife because you're attracted to a—a spoiled brat like Cynthia?"

"Did you—or anyone else—stop to consider why I might be attracted to a spoiled brat like Cynthia?" he countered bitterly. "Did it occur to you that I might find her attractive because she's not a snob? She doesn't hold my background against me. In fact, she gives every appearance of liking me."

"Cynthia likes anything in pants," Serena was stung to retaliate, tackling the buttons again, "particularly if he's paying the bills."

"And you're different?"

"More discriminating, anyway," she informed him, "and money never mattered to me until you and my father..." The words died on her lips when she realized how he was looking at her, a new awareness in his gaze as he followed each slight movement of her fingers—and something was different, she discovered. The balance of power between them had shifted; he wasn't the cool tormentor this time—*she* was—which meant, she understood now, that the attraction between them wasn't one-sided. That was knowledge she could use, she decided instantly, her heart beating faster, the desire for revenge so strong that she could almost taste it. "Money never mattered to me," she began again, still working on the buttons, forcing her fingers to move more slowly, deliberately prolonging the moment. "I knew nothing about that agreement between you and my father."

"So you keep telling me," he acknowledged almost absently, watching intently as she dispatched one more button, then another, "still playing the innocent..."

"I'm not playing."

"You seem to be at the moment."

"Well, I suppose..." She freed one more button, felt for the next and found nothing. Glancing down, she saw that she'd finished the job; her dress lay open all the way to the dropped waist, permitting a tantalizing glimpse of her satin and lace camisole. "Yes, perhaps I am," she admitted carelessly. "Should I stop?"

"I hope you won't," he told her, a slight roughness in his voice, "not yet."

"All right." Unconcerned, she shrugged; her dress slipped from one shoulder, and she heard his quick indrawn breath. He stood motionless, shoulders braced, a subtle tension in his stance, watching her—devouring her—with his dark and glittering gaze. At last! she thought, knowing the sweet balm of vindication, even triumph. Finally she had the upper hand; for once she was in control—a moment to prolong and fully savor before she extracted her revenge. Deliberately, she freed her other shoulder and heard the whisper of the fabric as it drifted slowly to the floor. "There. Satisfied?"

"Satisfied?" he murmured, one eyebrow rising. "What do you think?"

"I think you're going to have to be," she responded evenly. "The free show's over for tonight."

"Hardly free, sweetheart," he corrected, smiling, his self-possession instantly in place again. "I paid a lot for the right——"

"You have no rights here," she cut in firmly. "None at all!"

"But I do," he stated with deceptive mildness, "and I'm about to exercise them."

"But I don't want you to," she whispered, beginning to panic, wondering how he'd managed to get the upper hand again. "You wouldn't dare!"

"You know better than that," he objected lazily, but there was nothing lazy about him when he moved—like a sleek jungle cat, she thought, watching wide-eyed as he closed the space between them. "I've been patient long enough," he told her, so near that his breath stirred her hair. "Now I'm going to have what I paid for."

"No!" She took a step backward and found herself trapped between his powerful form and the side of the bed. "I won't let you!"

"You have no choice, sweetheart," he pointed out, laughing when he saw her outraged expression. "Did Daddy forget to tell you that he put no restrictions on the sale? You belong to me, Serena, every beautiful inch."

"Damn you!" Goaded beyond her endurance, she struck out at him, brought up short when he captured her wrist. "Stop it," she demanded, fighting him with all of her strength, pushing ineffectually against his chest with her free hand. Finally, in one last desperate effort, she twisted away, then felt herself falling, forced back onto the bed, the weight of his body holding her captive. "You can't do this, she raged. "I don't want——"

"You do want," he corrected carelessly, watching her face as he explored the curves hidden beneath satin and lace, his hands growing bolder, brushing lightly across her breasts then moving on. "Why else that little striptease act of yours?"

"It wasn't——"

"It was," he assured her, his hands returning to her breasts.

"No," she protested breathlessly, trying to close her mind to the magic of his caress. "I never meant—not this——"

"But you did," he corrected with brief economy, turning so that the weight of his body no longer held her in place. Now he was lying beside her, propped up on one arm in order to see her face, so sure of his power over her that the length of his body was barely in contact with hers. "You know you did," he murmured, only the clever work of his hand holding her captive. "From the very start we've both been wanting this."

No, he was wrong! she tried to tell herself, but an insidious languor was invading her body; it was hard even to concentrate. He was too clever for her, and he knew... knew her weakness, she acknowledged helplessly as he continued his subtle assault. He was playing an incredibly exciting game, his hand returning again and again to her breasts, lingering never quite long enough... toying with her, coaxing her to respond until her control snapped and she finally arched shamelessly into his touch.

"Yes, that's right... that's better, isn't it?" he teased, and then, moving slowly—unbearably slowly!—he caressed every inch from the delicate arch of her foot to the softness of her inner thigh. "And how about this?" he inquired, making an erotic game of releasing her garters and stroking away her silk stockings, destroying the last of her inhibitions.

"You're not being fair," she complained weakly, reaching out to him, frowning when she encountered the stiff formality of his dress shirt, "and your shirt's in the way..." Impatiently she worked the buttons free, finally able to push the shirt open.

"Ah... yes," he breathed when she'd managed to get it off, leaving her just long enough to shed the rest of his clothing. "There, this will be better," he promised returning to her.

But "better" wasn't the word, she discovered when he had dispensed with her camisole and half slip. There was nothing so tepid as "better" about how it felt to lie together, no barriers between them... to share the intense excitement—the fire!—of his flesh against hers... Could this be love? she found herself wondering. Could love grow where there was so much anger and misunderstanding? She wanted this to be love, but she couldn't be sure... not even sure that it mattered. Only John mattered now! "Oh, yes..." she whispered, possessed by an imperative need to touch him and taste him, to return to him some of the magic he was giving to her. "John, I never——"

"No words—not now," he commanded, his lips cleverly teasing at hers, a deliberate, erotic invasion. "Don't even think...for now, just let it happen."

No words, she agreed silently; they didn't need words—not now, when every kiss and caress said all that they needed to say. She was suddenly sensitized to each nuance of his body and her own, daring to tease and tempt him while his hands and his lips drew her even deeper into desire. Finally, in a world consisting only of sensation, he kindled an even greater need in her—one deeper, more intense than she could possibly have imagined. It spiraled through her body, piercing her, destroying the last of her defenses, carrying her to the very edge of sanity. "Please," she said on an unsteady breath, clinging to him. "John, please..."

He paused, poised just above her, watching her intently. "Serena?" he bit out, his voice strained and harsh. "Are you sure?"

"Yes!" Her hands moved restlessly to draw him into her; instinctively her body arched...anything she thought, to fill this aching void. "Yes—John, make love to me..."

Finally, then, he entered her, carrying her once more to the edge...and then beyond, into the mindless, raging vortex of their passion. Vaguely, in the last explosive instant, she heard his breathing, as ragged as her own, felt the force of his response in the endless moment when he gave her the completion she craved.

"Satisfied?" he asked her later, when the storm had finally past.

"Mmm..." She smiled contentedly, idly wondering, What kind of word is that? Satisfied? An empty word, incapable of describing how she felt. "Of course," she finally said, staring up at him. For the first time, she realized, she was seeing him unguarded—without the careful watchfulness and slight edge of tension she had never known were in his face until now, when they were gone. "More than satisfied," she admitted shyly.

"Good." He stirred, just enough to lie beside her, raising himself on one arm so that he could see her face. "This was...beyond my wildest expectations," he told her, his voice lazy and indulgent, "and you—you were fantastic." His finger brushed her cheek, lightly traced her profile. "We're going to do this often."

"I hope so," she confided, bolder now.

"Of course you do...bawdy little Pilgrim," he murmured, teasing her, his finger moving on, following the sweet curve of her smile, "so delightfully responsive, and such unexpected depths, so much fire..."

"Because of you." Her lips parted to the erotic pressure of his coaxing, she moistened them, dared to let her tongue touch his finger, then dared even more—admitted what surely must be the truth. "I love you."

Instantly his finger was withdrawn. "Not that, sweetheart," he advised, eyes narrowing. "Don't go too far."

"But it's true," she insisted, reaching for his hand, to draw it back to her. "I always have, but after this——"

"Spare me," he said, clear warning in his voice. "We both knew what we wanted to get from this marriage—and now we know we're compatible. Well, that's a plus, but don't try to make it more than it is."

"But it is more!" It was too late, she knew, to retreat; her only hope now was to make him believe. "I love you—can't you tell? I never could have...have done what I just did unless——"

"What is it with you?" he inquired coldly, only a spark of anger in his eyes. "If you can pretend it's love, does it make you feel less like a prostitute?"

"No!" She stared up at him, feeling sick. "It wasn't like that."

"I'd say it was," he objected cruelly. "I paid for you, and you performed. That wasn't love, sweetheart." He turned away, abandoning her by leaving the bed. "That was need," he told her as he started toward the dressing room, then gave the knife one final twist, "or possibly frustration."

CHAPTER EIGHT

PLEASE, let it have been a dream...or a nightmare. Serena came awake with the thought fully formed, knew instantly its impossibility. She lay in a wild tangle of sheets and blankets; no need to wonder if last night had been real. If there had been any doubt in her mind, John's particular scent—that intensely masculine combination of soap, astringent after-shave and something powerfully physical—clung to the sheets, inviting her to remember.

Well, she wasn't going to remember, she vowed, sitting up in bed, hastily snatching the sheet to hide her nakedness. There was no point in remembering anything—except the way he had left her, and his killing words. He had used her; no better way to describe it than that. He had used her, and—even worse—he was determined to believe that she had merely used him.

He hadn't wanted to hear her declaration; there was no room for love in this farce of a marriage. He didn't want love. He wanted to believe that her motives were as cold-blooded and calculating as his. Their marriage was a tidy business arrangement, a merger...no, not a merger, she decided. A merger permitted at least the possibility that the two parties involved were equals, and in John's mind that possibility didn't exist. Instead, he had managed to pull off a hostile takeover; there was no room for equality—much less love!—in that kind of relationship.

Last night there had been a brief moment when—fool that she was!—she'd believed there was love between them. In her naïveté she'd assumed... Well, it was hard

131

to know just what she had assumed, and in the cold light of morning it made her uncomfortable to think about what had happened during the night. Still, it had felt—at least to her—that they had been making love, not just using each other. It was still hard to believe that something that felt so good and so right wasn't love—which proved how little she knew!

After all, she was hardly an expert, she admitted, leaning her aching head on her drawn-up knees. What she knew about making love—about *sex* she quickly corrected—was limited to last night and that long Fourth of July evening when they had come so close . . . and had there really been so much difference between those two nights? Perhaps so; on the Fourth of July there had been—she searched for the word—lightness, she finally concluded; lightness, and teasing, and laughter . . .

"They never set off enough to please me," John had told her as they'd sat together near the top of his hill, a perfect spot for viewing the town's grand fireworks show. Not that they had been paying close attention, Serena remembered; they'd been too busy watching each other to care much about the display in the sky. "I always want more—enough to fill the sky and go on all night. I want it all."

"You're too greedy," she chided, turning to study his profile. "No one can have it all."

"I can," he stressed, but his voice was threaded with laughter. "I always get what I want."

"Always? No way! Nearly always, perhaps," she conceded generously, and saw his lips quirk in amusement, "because you're a very capable man."

"Only capable?" he asked hopefully.

"Well . . ." she slanted her head to one side, pretending to give the matter serious thought " . . . you do have a certain charm."

"It's not charm, it's technique," he corrected with a broad smile. "For example——" He moved without warning; suddenly one arm was on either side of her, his hands splayed on the grass, bracing him while he held her captive "—what I want now is you...and I've got you. That's technique, my girl."

"That's not technique," she objected, still treating the whole thing as a joke—not that it still felt like a joke, she acknowledged. How could it, when he was so close, his breath stirring her hair, his clean male scent all around her? "It's brute force."

"Brute force?" he demanded with injured dignity. "I haven't laid a hand on you."

"True enough," she allowed breathlessly, instantly wishing he would lay a hand on her—even better, both hands, she decided, "but you've got me trapped," she pointed out, pretending a composure that was miles away from the truth. He had destroyed her composure; now she felt as though she was poised—precariously—at the edge of some deep and unknown chasm, some equally deep and unknown feeling building within her. "But still, I think it would be——"

"Are you sure? Is this brute force?" he inquired, his teeth catching lightly at her lower lip, his tongue teasing with hers. "Or this?" he continued, molding her to him, the heat of his body searing hers as they fell together, onto the grass. "Or this?" he persisted, one clever finger tracing the curve of her shoulder, finding the racing pulse at the base of her throat. "Don't tell me this is brute force!"

Of course she hadn't; she'd been so caught up in the magic his hands and his lips were creating that she hadn't said anything, hadn't even been able to think...

He had made love to her that night, she told herself now in the clear light of an October morning; surely he had! Or was it simply that he had seduced her? Certainly, he had been—what? Not the aggressor, she acknowledged. There had been nothing aggressive about his actions, but he had been very much in control of the situation, and of her...

"Incredible...incredibly lovely," she'd heard him murmur, and had only then realized that somehow he'd disposed of her cotton shift and the lacy scraps she'd been wearing beneath. "No—it's all right, my love," he'd coaxed, catching her hands when she would have tried to cover herself. "You're so lovely to look at...my sweet Puritan, there's no need to be shy."

"I'm not a Puritan," she objected halfheartedly, and not quite so shy, she discovered when he released her hands, and—this time—she lay submissive beneath his glittering gaze. "I'm a Pilgrim several generations removed," she explained, discovering that talking was a way to avoid thinking about what seemed to be happening. "The Puritans were the terribly proper ones—inhibited, I suppose——" she broke off briefly, watched wide-eyed as John began to remove his shirt, then hurried on "—but the Pilgrims weren't...like that... Some of them were—very bawdy."

"Is that a fact?" he inquired, casting his shirt aside, lying down next to her. "And what about you, I wonder?" he murmured, drawing her close. "Let's see what you are..." He bent his head, his lips seeking her breast, laughing softly when she instinctively arched toward him. "That's right, my bawdy Pilgrim..."

For a while it had been magic. The last of the fireworks had faded from the sky and the dark silence around them had been disturbed only by his soft laughter and whispered endearments, her quick, uneven breathing as he found even bolder ways to tease and tempt her, until...

"Darling Serena...my own bawdy Pilgrim," John had murmured, his voice unsteady, even ragged. "Lord, there's no turning back now..."

That had stopped her dead in her tracks, suddenly all too aware of the enormity of what was happening. "No! I can't," she'd told him.

And how he must have laughed, she thought now, sitting alone in his bed, wrapped in a sheet. She'd been the worst kind of terrified virgin that night; it must have been almost more than he could manage—to keep from laughing when she'd scrambled away from him to hunt frantically for her clothing.

Of course he hadn't let her know what he was thinking. "Serena, sweetheart, it's all right," he'd reassured her, his voice tinged with understanding and affection. "We don't have to—not yet. Lord, I didn't mean . . . This is all too new for you, isn't it?"

She had nodded, afraid to speak, tears gathering behind her eyelids. If only he wouldn't be so nice! she had despaired. She could have handled his anger—it wouldn't have been the first time a man had been angry with her for calling things to a halt, although in fairness she had been forced to admit that she'd never given another man an excuse to be anything approaching as angry as John had the right to be.

She had known enough about how men were made to understand that she had been unspeakably irresponsible in letting things go as far as they had. It had been a wonder—and, she supposed, a tribute to John's powers of self-control—that he'd been able to stop himself when she'd finally come to her senses. She had deserved his anger that night, and a towering rage would have been easier to bear than kindness and understanding.

Well, last night had been very different! Serena acknowledged, caught up in the anger—and the sadness—memory had left behind. Last night she hadn't played the role of terrified virgin; she'd been willing—no, she corrected, scrupulously honest, she'd been much more than willing! She'd been eager and unafraid—but only because she'd wanted to believe that there must be some love present between them. She'd felt it strongly enough to admit it. In return, though, John had trampled her feelings. She supposed that knowing he hadn't believed her was a blessing. It meant that she at least had her pride, but pride wasn't what she had wanted. She had wanted love, John's love——

"Oh! I didn't know..."

Serena jumped a mile, then raised her head, struck dumb at the sight of Mrs. Hutchins, cleaning supplies in hand.

"I didn't realize..." The housekeeper stared back, obviously as shocked as Serena. "I assumed you'd have left by now."

"No. That is——" Lord, Professor Brandenson would have been sailing on for hours now, Serena realized, and she hadn't even thought about going in to school; nor did she care—not after what had happened last night! "—I won't be going in today. I'm not feeling well."

"Then I'm sure you'd rather that I waited——" Mrs. Hutchins broke off to inspect the room, and her expression, never very revealing, in Serena's opinion, grew positively wooden "—to do this room some other time. Or would you like...shall I straighten it up a bit for you?"

"No, don't bother. I would like——" Serena stopped dead when she saw what had caused the housekeeper's peculiar reaction. "I'd like some coffee, if you don't mind," she forced herself to continue, hoping her embarrassment wasn't showing. "Black," she added as Mrs. Hutchins turned and headed out of the door—probably as glad to get away as Serena was to have her gone.

What must she be thinking? Serena wondered, alone again. Her clothes and John's lay scattered on the floor; hers soft drifts of maroon, his—emphatic and uncompromising—black and white, the gold chain a glittering contrast. It looked, she decided, dismayed, as though some kind of mini-orgy had taken place in this room, as though the two of them hadn't wasted a second in shedding their clothes. It was a wonder that Mrs. Hutchins had been able to hide her reaction behind a proper mask—given that the poor woman knew her employers had been living completely separate lives since their wedding. In fact, just a couple of days before she'd made who knew how many trips up and down the stairs, carrying all of Serena's things into this room, carefully hanging clothes in the wardrobe, filling the dresser drawers. And now all this clothing was strewn about...

And you are not going to make a mad dash to hide everything! Serena lectured herself, angry for caring, for actually having considered the idea. Even if she'd wanted to it was too late, because the housekeeper was back with the coffee.

"If there's anything else you'd like," she offered, placing the tray on the table beside the bed. "Some breakfast, perhaps?"

"No, thanks," Serena responded with forced carelessness, "this is fine."

"Then I'll get back to work." Mrs. Hutchins made for the door, this time taking pains not to look too closely at the rest of the room. "But I wonder..." she paused in the doorway, turning back to Serena "...has your sister left for good? I assumed that I would be told when——"

"Cynthia?" Serena interrupted to ask—stupidly, she realized immediately, as though she had several sisters tucked away in this little house. "Isn't she still in her room? She usually sleeps very late."

"The room is empty." The housekeeper's expression was still correctly wooden, only her dark eyes alive with curiosity. Something—quite a bit, actually—has been going on here, and I'd love to know what, those eyes seemed to say. "She certainly slept late enough yesterday, but she was gone when I got here this morning, and it doesn't appear that she left anything behind. Still, I thought...perhaps she is coming back?"

"I have no idea," Serena said coolly, ignoring the unspoken question—if your sister is gone, will you be moving back into the guest room...? Will John let me? That's the real question, Serena knew, but her mind skittered away from that thought. "She didn't tell me her plans. Perhaps Mr. Bourque will know. I'll ask him when he gets home."

"And in the meantime," Mrs. Hutchins prompted, "shall I at least clean the room?"

"Why don't you do that?" Deliberately, Serena turned away—carefully, so as not to disturb the sheet keeping her decent—to pour coffee, hoping Mrs. Hutchins would take the hint.

She finally did, and Serena was permitted a few minutes alone with her dark thoughts before the next interruption.

"No, please don't bother. I'll just go up."

Lillian's voice, Serena registered, wondering how she'd missed the warning of the brass door knocker, listening now to Lillian's light footsteps on the stairs, then her brisk tap at the bedroom door.

"Yes, just a minute," Serena called out, with time only to unwrap herself from the sheet and grab for a robe—no time, she realized, to pick up John's clothes or her own, the damning evidence of last night. "Come in."

"Thank you." Lillian swept into the room, as impeccably turned out as ever: gray tweed skirt, matching jacket worn over a silvery silk blouse, just the right jewelry, every blond hair in place. Only her expression—the tiny frown lines on her forehead, the unnaturally tense muscles around her mouth—hinted that something was wrong. "Serena, I don't understand," Lillian began, wasting no time on small talk. "Mrs. Hutchins says that Cynthia isn't here."

"Yes, I——"

"But I must try to stop her," Lillian cut in, as close to wringing her hands as Serena had ever seen her, "before she does something incredibly foolish! Serena, where is she?"

"I don't know," Serena offered inadequately, and the muscles around Lillian's mouth grew even tighter.

"But you must know! You take her in, encourage her in this... this rebellion of hers—and now you say you don't know where she is?" Lillian demanded on a rising note, then drew a deep breath and continued more calmly, "Serena, it's irresponsible for you to play with her future this way... I just don't understand why..."

"I wasn't," Serena insisted, retreating to perch on the edge of the bed. "It was John's idea."

"John's?" Lillian repeated, incredulous. "What does John have to do with Cynthia?"

A lot more than you might think, Serena was tempted to say, but she wasn't about to discuss her wild imaginings, or what Cynthia had said about John. Besides, Serena reflected, she knew with absolute certainty that nothing had happened between John and Cynthia last night. "When you and Dad told her to go back to Houston, she went to see John," Serena explained, sticking to facts, "and John said she could stay with us for a while."

"But why?" Lillian asked, the rising, edge-of-control note back in her voice. "Why would he get involved?"

"I don't know." Serena shrugged. "He said that he wanted to make sure that she didn't do anything foolish."

"Then he should have told her to go back to Gregory," Lillian snapped. "He should have forced her to go!"

"I don't think that would have been wise," Serena began carefully. "She really wasn't in any mood to be forced to do anything."

Lillian practically snorted at that. "Of course not! You made it so easy for her—having her here, taking her out

to parties...she was free to do whatever she pleased!
Why on earth would she do what was sensible with the
two of you indulging her? By now she's probably ruined
her chances with Gregory."

"John has been making sure that she doesn't," Serena
offered quickly. "He's been lecturing——"

"John," Lillian scoffed. She turned away to work off
some of her agitation by pacing, her efforts hampered
first by Serena's half slip, then John's dress shirt. "What
good did it do to have John lecturing?" she demanded,
carefully stepping around the clothing on the floor. "It's
not as though he gives a damn! Honestly, Serena, why
did you let him get involved——?"

"I didn't know what he'd done. I'd been away, and
didn't get home until he'd already asked——"

"Well, when you did know," Lillian persisted, eyes
blazing, "you could have done something! Why didn't
you make him stop being involved?"

"I couldn't," Serena retorted, stung by the injustice
of Lillian's attitude. "I'm in no position to tell John
what he can and can't do. Perhaps you've forgotten, but
we don't have the world's most normal marriage."

"No?" Lillian turned back to her, eyebrows arching.
"If this is anything to go by——" one gray kid shoe
gently stirred first the half slip, then John's shirt "—I'd
say you had a reasonably normal marriage—more...
uninhibited than many, perhaps, but certainly...
intimate!"

"And what good does that do?" Serena asked, revealing more bitterness than she'd intended, but the
memory of the previous night was still too painful to
hide. "It doesn't give me any rights in this marriage."

"No?" Lillian was suddenly thoughtful, Cynthia's
problems briefly forgotten or at least shelved. "Not
rights, precisely, but that's not really the issue..." She
drew the rocking chair closer to the bed, positioning it
so that when she sat down she was directly facing Serena.

"My dear, haven't you learned? When you're married to a man, and intimate with him, that intimacy gives you certain...opportunities. As a wife, there are things you can say, discussions you can have after...when he's more...receptive—well, I don't need to spell it out, do I?"

"You would for John. We don't have that kind of relationship," Serena said shortly. "I'm not his wife. I'm just a possession. He bought my name, bought into an old, proper Boston family——"

"Serena!" Lillian's voice, clear and very firm, cut through Serena's painful recital. "You can't spend your life holding that against him!"

"He doesn't give me much choice! He holds it against me, throws it in my face all the time... If only..." Serena's voice wavered briefly "...if only Dad hadn't done it."

"My dear, he had no choice," Lillian countered, although she did have the grace to sound distressed. "It wasn't as though he wanted it that way, but things were going very badly for him at the time... It really was the only way out."

"John said it wasn't that bad," Serena objected. "He said it wasn't anything that Dad could have gone to jail for, just that he would have lost face."

"There was a bit more to it than that," Lillian rebutted crisply. "Your father was investing for himself and for a few friends. If he hadn't been able to cover his losses it would have affected a number of people."

"His friends, and his own bank account, were more important than his daughter?" Serena asked bitterly. "That's why I'm in this mess?"

"If it is it's a mess of your own choosing," Lillian retaliated. "You were determined to marry John. You wouldn't listen to reason——"

"And, once Dad had cut the deal, he didn't care!"

"Of course he cared! He still does. You must never think that he doesn't!"

"He has a strange way of showing it! Until he realized that there was something in it for him he was dead set against my marrying John—it was too soon, John wasn't the right sort, not to be trusted... Lil, you know what he said. He was absolutely furious—I've never seen him so angry."

"But that wasn't——" Lillian broke off, biting her lip. "Oh, my dear—if you just understood."

"What I understand is that I'm stuck with this farce of a marriage, and I'll never be happy—John won't let me be happy." Serena paused, staring down at her wide wedding band, heavy on her finger, weighting it down... an appropriate symbol of her marriage, she thought, and then drew a deep breath and asked carefully, "What would happen now if I got a divorce?"

"But you wouldn't," Lillian countered sharply. "You couldn't!"

"Why not?" Serena asked in a cold, hard voice.

"Because——" Lillian stopped, shaking her head, as though she didn't know where to begin. "There's the money, for one thing. At the very least, John would want it returned, and your father couldn't possibly... It's all spent, to cover the debts. He couldn't raise that kind of money, and it will be years before he makes it back."

"What if I paid John back?" Serena asked, her mind suddenly clear, her thoughts focused on one objective. "I get the principal of my mother's trust fund in a couple of years. I could borrow against it—or wait, I suppose, if I had to."

"But I don't think..." Lillian's hands fluttered helplessly. "I don't know what the trust fund is worth. It might not be enough...and your father wouldn't let you do it. He never even considered trying to use it when things began to go bad. And besides, even if it could be arranged, and your father agreed, I don't think money's the real problem. It's what John would do, what he would say...

"He knows everything, Serena! He refused to even consider giving your father the money unless he knew why, and your father—well, he felt it only fair to be completely honest——"

"With John," Serena pointed out coldly, "but not with me!"

"He hoped you'd never know," Lillian offered inadequately. "You were so much in love... Your father wasn't so sure about John, and he honestly thought that this agreement might help."

"Help?" Serena demanded shrilly. "He thought it would help if he sold me?"

"He thought it would help to put things on a clear business basis...that John would be good to you—make you happy—to protect his investment, that——"

"No!" Serena got up from the bed and slipped by Lillian to go to the window. "That's it," she said, staring down into the dying garden. "I don't want to hear any more! If Dad really thought he could—could reduce me to that—an investment to be protected!—then I don't want to hear any more...

"The one time in my life I needed him to protect me..." she said dully—no pain yet, she reflected; at the moment she felt only isolation and emptiness. The pain, she knew, would come later. "The one time when it really counted to have him on my side...and where was he? Cutting a deal, selling me to the highest bidder."

"That's not true, Serena," Lillian countered forcefully. "Your father has always—always!—been there for you. You can't know...you don't understand."

"But I do," Serena corrected almost gently. "I know that I don't need to stay in this marriage—I can get a divorce. I don't need to keep Dad's dirty secret...not after he's spent all these years—my lifetime!—pretending to love me."

"Pretending? Perhaps," Lillian conceded, her tone revealing an intensity of emotion, "but not pretending to love you. That was always an absolute. He's loved you so much, all these years, that he's been willing to pretend that you're his daughter."

"His daughter?" Serena repeated on a questioning note, finally turning away from the window to face her stepmother again. "What do you mean?"

"That you aren't! Your mother...there was always someone else for her...almost from the start."

"Who?" Serena demanded, focusing on what appeared to be the one tangible in this glimpse of a new and alien world.

Lillian shook her head. "It wasn't just one. There were a great many, one after another. He—your father..." she paused awkwardly "...well, he didn't—after the first few he stopped trying to find out. She wasn't well, Serena. Your father knew there had been problems for her while she was growing up. Her parents were very cold, and your father thought...it was as though she couldn't help herself. She just had to keep looking for love."

"But..." Serena stopped, attempting to order her thoughts. The funny thing was, she reflected, that she believed Lillian—not for any specific, concrete reason, but because it was obvious that Lillian wasn't making it up. The halting cadence with which she was telling the story had nothing to do with the need to think up additional lies; it was a reflection of Lillian's discomfort, her reluctance to tell warring with her determination to tell the whole truth. "If...she was like that, why didn't he divorce her?"

"Because...he had grounds, of course, and there was no love—either way, not after the very beginning—but he represented security for her. He was someone to come home to each time she got hurt—and she always got hurt. And he felt he couldn't abandon her—she was so un-

happy—desperately so. He felt responsible for her—and
for you, too, once you were born.''

"But, if he stayed,'' Serena began, working her way
through the tangle, "how can he be sure that I'm
not... not his child?''

"Because... Oh, Serena, this is terribly hard,'' Lillian
confessed, "but he'd met me, and...long enough before
you were born, he and I...well, he wouldn't leave her,
but he was being faithful to me. There was no possibility—none at all—but that didn't change how he felt
about you from the start. He was determined—no
hesitation!—to be your father.''

"Which is why you told me... and why I can't——''
Serena stopped and closed her eyes, briefly reluctant to
face the truth "—I can't, can I?'' she continued, her
eyes open again, looking not at Lillian, but beyond—
into a lonely future. "I can't divorce John, can't run
the risk of what he would do to... to my father.''

"I hope you won't,'' Lillian allowed, her voice carefully devoid of expression, trying not to apply any more
pressure, Serena realized. "You don't need me to tell
you that he'd be hurt.''

"No, and I think it would be—I don't know!—dis-
illusioning, perhaps... Wouldn't it shake his faith in
himself if, all those years after he made the decision to
protect me, I refused to do the same for him?''

"I think it would,'' Lillian agreed, "but I've already
said too much.''

"No, you've said just enough,'' Serena assured her
with a painful attempt at a smile. "I know what I've got
to do—what I can't do,'' she corrected. "I've got to make
the best of this marriage.''

"And I think—I really believe that you can. There's
obviously attraction between you...'' She paused to
survey the scattered clothing, a smile actually tugging at
the corners of her mouth "...spontaneity too, and that's
not a bad place to begin.''

Serena shook her head. "I don't think so. John doesn't think much of Dad for what he did, and even less of me. He's an unforgiving man."

"It's his pride," Lillian suggested with the air of one speaking from experience. "His kind of success, in a city like Boston, will have exposed him to a lot of unpleasantness, and this arrangement with your father must seem like more of the worst kind of behavior. Still, given time," she continued determinedly, "I think he'll begin to soften."

"Yes," Serena agreed tonelessly. There was no point in arguing—that would only make Lillian feel worse—but Serena knew that John wouldn't soften. None of his buildings were crumbling, and his pride and his anger were constructed with the same strength and determination. No, John wouldn't soften, but perhaps she would harden...given time.

There was an unpleasant word for what she was, Serena reflected after Lillian's departure, but the whole idea had no real meaning. Intellectually, Serena could grasp the reality that she was not her father's daughter, but it was hard to believe, hard to *feel* that she wasn't when he'd done such a marvelous job of making her feel that she was.

All those years! she mused. For all those years he'd unconditionally accepted her—now there's irony for you! she told herself. She, who had always despised the effort to maintain appearances, was the beneficiary of an incredibly effective effort to do just that. She wasn't Serena Winslow Wright, named—cosmic joke!—for her father's mother. Instead she was...who could know? All that could be said was that she was her mother's love child— that much was sure—and some unknown man's... bastard.

Oh, the irony! Serena thought; there was even more of it than she had realized—more than just the pretense of her life. There was also her marriage: John had bought

Serena Winslow Wright—who didn't exist! He'd paid for a blood connection to one of the most proper of Boston families—when there was no blood connection... Well, there was still her mother, Serena conceded, but her mother's family was—in the general scheme of things—pretty unimpressive. The Tiptons were connected—but not well-connected—to the best Boston families. No, the real social clout—what John had wanted so badly—belonged to the Winslows and the Wrights—and she was neither.

Another irony! she realized. She had talked of divorcing John and now knew she couldn't, but he could divorce her. Perhaps he would if she told him the truth... but she knew she couldn't do that either. She was well and truly trapped—no way could she betray the man she'd always thought of as her father! He'd guarded the secret of her birth, loved her without reservation, given her a home and the illusion of a family. Only once, at the end of that memorable Fourth of July evening, had he ever been truly—toweringly—angry with her. At the time she hadn't understood, but now—thanks to Lillian—Serena thought she could see the reasons behind her father's extreme reaction.

CHAPTER NINE

FOR Serena and John, the world had exploded without any warning. In the dark hour before dawn they had been hand in hand, halfway up the drive when Serena's father had appeared in the doorway.

"Where the devil have you been?" he'd thundered— like the outraged Victorian father in a bad melodrama, Serena had thought, forced to control the urge to laugh. "And who is this man? Not, I think, the schoolboy you've been telling us about. You've been lying to us, haven't you?" he'd finished with furious distaste.

Serena's urge to laugh had died. There was going to be a scene, she'd realized instantly, a desperately unpleasant one, and all because she'd made the mistake of keeping John a secret.

It had been an impulsive, poorly thought-out decision. Lillian had expressed disapproval of the man, and Serena had wanted to avoid the possibility of unpleasantness—but only for a little while, she had promised herself. If seeing him developed into something serious there would be time enough to carefully break the news to her father and Lillian, dispel their concerns, talk them out of their undoubted disapproval... When that had been accomplished she could safely have John meet them.

In the meantime she'd been stretching her powers of invention to the limit. Satisfying family curiosity about her suddenly busy social life had been the easy part. She'd simply invented a former college classmate, making up stories about him in answer to any questions. With John she'd been forced to manufacture a series of ex-

cuses—some ingenious, some patently absurd—to keep
him from coming to the house.

Her system had been working perfectly for two weeks
now; she'd had no reason to think it wouldn't keep on
working perfectly—even tonight, when she'd broken her
own rule by agreeing to let John take her home. Why
not? she'd thought when he'd suggested it. The idea made
sense—she didn't have her car with her because she'd
walked across the fields to John's place once Lillian's
party was in full swing. He hadn't wanted her walking
back alone so late at night—which was, she'd thought,
precisely why she didn't need to worry. It was nearly
four in the morning; her father, Lillian, and Cynthia
were bound to be asleep... but they hadn't been, and it
was obvious from her father's expression that her
harmless scheme had blown up in her face.

"Have you no shame?" he demanded, ignoring John
to glare at her. "Leaving the party—sneaking away!—
without a word to anyone, staying out all night——"

"Not quite all night," Serena put in quickly—a
mistake, she realized instantly.

"Not quite... as though that makes a difference! I
never thought I'd see the day when I'd be ashamed to
have you as a daughter—behaving like a tramp!"

"That isn't true," John said quietly, but with a hint
of steel beneath his words. "I think you're overreacting."

"And who the hell are you to tell me anything?"

"John Bourque, sir." He offered his hand—all civ-
ilized politeness, Serena noted. "I can explain."

"I doubt it," Ted Wright snapped, pointedly ignoring
John's outstretched hand. "So you're Bourque?" With
an expression of acute displeasure he studied the younger
man. "Well, you can leave now. This is a family matter,
and I'll deal with my daughter!" He pushed open the
screen door, came down the drive to seize Serena's arm,
propelling her into the house. "There will be no more

of this kind of behavior—doing goodness knows what, and with a man like that!''

The criticism of John, no matter how vague, stung at Serena. "A man like what?'' she demanded, stopping just inside the door, turning to confront her father. "You don't know——''

"I know that he's up to no good, and you've been happy to oblige,'' Ted retorted, forcing her to keep moving, not releasing her arm until she was inside the living room.

She stood alone, briefly closing her eyes against lights too bright after the darkness outside. When she opened them she saw that her father had joined Lillian by the fireplace, the two of them a study in contrast—her father still murderously angry, Lillian concerned and anxious.

"My dear, how could you?'' she asked unhappily. "And with that dreadful man...''

"He is not a dreadful man,'' Serena snapped. "Just because you don't like him——''

"Whether I like him or not isn't the issue,'' Lillian offered, attempting to inject a reasonable note, "but I can have a little objectivity. You can't, not when he's——''

"Seduced you,'' Ted Wright thundered, jumping back in. "Lord, he—he's defiled you!''

"That's not true, Mr. Wright.''

Serena watched—it was like watching a scene filmed in slow motion—as Lillian's head and her father's turned, seeing for the first time the tall figure framed in the doorway.

"What the devil are you doing here?'' Serena's father demanded. "I didn't invite you into my house.''

"I realize that, but I felt I should be here,'' John agreed evenly, his voice calm and unhurried—the only sane one in the room, Serena thought, relieved. "This concerns me as much as it does Serena.''

"Yes, you'd like to think that, wouldn't you?" her father inquired sourly. "You've been busy—laying a trap for her, seducing her..."

"Not at all." John dismissed that idea with one of those quick gestures Serena had come to know so well. "I want to marry her."

Marry? He wanted to marry her! That was what he'd said, Serena realized, but her father's fresh explosion gave her no time to absorb the magnitude of John's quiet announcement.

"Marry her?" Serena's father shouted. "You can't marry her! Who the hell do you think you are, to say you're going to marry her?"

"I love her," John responded evenly, "and I believe she loves me."

"You think... I'm sure you've made her think so," Ted came back savagely, "but I won't permit it! I know what it is—you found her weakness!"

What weakness? Serena wondered, now thoroughly bewildered. This scene was making no sense at all— John's declaration, when she hadn't even been sure he would keep on seeing her... her father's reaction, the terrible anger, the shouting... She shivered, all the anger making her feel sick. She wasn't used to anger, didn't know how to handle it. She'd grown up in a house remarkably free of anger, had never heard her father raise his voice. Cynthia sometimes had her little sulky tantrums; Lillian sometimes grew impatient and snapped at someone—but that was all! Serena couldn't remember anything like this; her beloved father never got angry, never shouted, never said cruel or hurtful things...but suddenly this most placid and even-tempered of men was a raging tyrant! "Daddy, please," she began, unconsciously falling back on the habits of childhood, "it's not like that. I love John."

"You can't say that," he thundered, his anger blazing out at her. "You don't know, can't understand! You're

in such a state—that man has put you in such a state—
that you're not thinking clearly."

"I can. I am!"

"Nonsense! I can see how you spent the night," her
father bit out, eyeing her with extreme distaste, "what
you let this man do to you—what you did with him.
Look at yourself!"

Involuntarily her gaze was drawn to the antique mirror
over the fireplace. She looked positively wanton, she
acknowledged, unable to prevent the flush of color which
stained her cheeks. Her hair was wild, tumbling around
her face; her cotton shift was grass-stained, badly
creased, and—worst of all—the top three buttons had
been left undone, permitting an almost indecent view of
the creamy swell of her breasts.

"Exactly," her father said after a long moment. "It's
not a pretty sight, is it? What this man has made of
you..."

"I——" She swallowed, attempting to ease the hard
lump of fear in her throat, then cast a quick, desperate
glance at John, wishing he would say something, find
some way...but he wasn't going to help, she finally
understood. He was silent and very still—waiting,
watching her with a burning gaze. Why? Did he expect
her to settle this? "Daddy..." she began again, twisting
her hands, fighting to stay calm and failing miserably.
"Daddy, it doesn't matter what happened tonight. John
and I—we're in love, and if he wants...I'm going to
marry him."

"No! Not with my blessing," her father raged. "If
you give in to this—this weakness you'll be no daughter
of mine!"

"Oh, Ted," Lillian said unhappily, reaching for his
hand. "You don't mean that!"

"Of course I do," he snapped—her father, snapping
at Lillian? Serena asked herself, shocked to the core to
see him brush away Lillian's hand. "Don't interfere."

This was awful—worse than awful, Serena knew, blinking quickly against the tears which threatened. Things were out of control—her father was out of control!—for reasons beyond her comprehension, but it was obvious that nothing was going to be solved tonight. How could it be when her father was beyond reason?

"John," she began, turning to him, needing to buy some time, "let me—give me...I don't know...a few days, I think."

"Serena, you don't need this," he countered, his gaze still burning. "You can come with me—right now."

"No." She shook her head, ignoring the hand he held out to her. "I—it can't be like this! I think—I just need a little time... Please?"

She waited, holding her breath, her eyes imploring him to understand all that she couldn't explain. Around her it was very still, her father waiting, Lillian waiting, the room itself...all waiting for John's answer.

"All right," he finally said, inclining his head in a brief sign of assent, "if that's what you want. You know how to get in touch with me."

That scene made perfect sense now, Serena reflected, sitting alone in the middle of John's bed. Her father's anger, those cryptic references to her weakness...he'd been afraid that she was beginning to take after her mother. Small wonder, given the way events had transpired to make it look that way! Serena had been hiding John's existence, just as she supposed her mother had hidden her affairs. To compound the problem, fate had decreed that her father would discover her secret on the one night when Serena must have looked the way her mother would have looked after spending time with one of her lovers.

Her father, she thought now, must have believed that the past was coming back to haunt him. In that early morning hour he probably hadn't been focusing on Serena; he'd been remembering his wife. Once, if only for a brief time, he must have loved her deeply. At least once, before he'd given up and found at least a measure of happiness with Lillian, he might have confronted Serena's mother with the same fury with which he'd confronted Serena—with some of the same words, too, she was willing to bet.

It had counted for nothing, that night, that Serena had been a good daughter for twenty-five years, that she'd never been wild, that her few relationships with men had been safe and decorous—in fact, pretty bloodless and dull! That night, Serena was sure, her father had been emotionally confused; briefly she had been not his daughter, but his wife.

Unfortunately, it was a confusion he'd been un-willing—or unable—to give up. For nearly a week Serena had kept trying to talk to him about John, choosing her times carefully, hoping to find him in a good mood . . . without success. Ted Wright had been beyond an appeal to reason—locked, Serena suspected now, in the misery of his first marriage, working through feelings he must have repressed or ignored when they were new.

At the time, though, Serena had understood none of this. She'd only known that, in her father's eyes, she was a disappointment. Worse than that, she'd known that her father's forgiveness would come slowly . . . if at all, she'd added mentally, then instantly rejected such a thought.

Of course he would forgive her! she'd assured herself; how could he not? She'd always been his favorite—just as Cynthia had always been Lillian's. At the time, though, the issue had seemed to threaten the very fabric of the family, affecting not only Serena's relationship with her father, but also his relationship with Lillian. Surprisingly, for one who had called John "that dreadful man," Lillian had tried to be on Serena's side; the few times Lillian had attempted to intervene she had met with the same hostility...

"It's insane," Serena tried explaining to John when, tired of waiting for her to contact him, he'd come to see her while no one else was home, "but he won't even listen to reason. He refuses to even consider——" She broke off then, turning away so that John wouldn't see the tears welling in her eyes.

"Serena, sweetheart," he soothed, slipping his arms around her waist, drawing her back against him, "this is what he wants—don't you see? He wants to destroy us."

"No, I don't think so." She shook her head. "It's something else, I'm sure...and if I could just get through to him..."

"He could make you spend a lifetime trying to get through to him—delays and threats, more scenes like the one the other night."

"Not that." Within the circle of his arms Serena turned to face him. "He's never been like that before—he never gets angry! Dad's way is to be reasonable, to talk things out and settle them...which is why I think there must be something more to this."

"Of course there is, sweetheart," John told her, an angry glitter in his eyes. "He doesn't approve of me. I'm not good enough for his little girl."

"Don't say that—ever," she protested sharply. "It's not true, and it's not the way my father thinks. He's not like that! I know it's something else—I just don't know what!"

"Does it really matter?"

"Of course it matters! I hate the way things are right now."

"So do I," he agreed almost absently, drawing her closer. "Sweetheart, I want you with me...all the time," he continued, his voice an intimate murmur now. "I want you with me every day and every night..." his lips brushed her cheek "...I burn for you," he finished as his mouth closed over hers.

He kissed her with a single-minded thoroughness, penetrating her reserve, demanding her response—nothing gentle, nothing subtle about this kiss, she realized, briefly shocked before the tide of need and passion captured her. Just like the other night, she thought as her fingers tangled in his hair and her body grew more pliant, molding itself instinctively into the taut lines of his. Just like the other night...and only John can make me feel this way... "Only you," she whispered when she could.

"And only you, sweetheart," he answered with a lazy smile. "This is so good——" his lips briefly tasted hers and then withdrew "—so real." His lips returned, this time to tease at hers. "Sweetheart, don't let this end."

"I couldn't," she confessed, and felt his smile against her lips.

"Then marry me," he coaxed. "Come with me now...forget about your father."

"I can't," she whispered sadly, withdrawing slightly. "Not like this."

"Of course you can," he objected lightly. "It's so simple——"

"For you, perhaps, but not for me," she snapped, then shocked them both by bursting into tears. "You don't understand," she told him, her voice muffled against his shirt when he drew her back to him—gently this time, one hand smoothing back her hair. "We've always been a family, and we've never fought, and now it's terrible. When Lillian tries to help he's angry with her too. It's as though I've ruined things."

"Serena, you haven't ruined things," John countered urgently. "You've fallen in love and you want to get married—nothing wrong with that."

"But if I just walk out it will be wrong," she insisted brokenly. "I've got to try to make him understand... stop being quite so angry. Please, John?"

"Are you asking for more time?" he asked, a strange expression in his eyes.

She nodded. "Just a little bit?"

"And if that doesn't work?"

"It will. It's got to! Things won't go on like this forever," she promised.

"Yes...well, we'll see, won't we?" he inquired coolly. "How long, sweetheart? Another week?"

"I suppose," she agreed uncertainly... but she hadn't needed that much time. Before the week was up her father had relented and given his approval—but not until John had gone to him, asking him to name his price.

That brief scene, Serena realized, still sitting motionless in the middle of John's bed, had started all the trouble. Her father's reaction by itself wouldn't have caused any damage. It was her second plea to John for more time which had ruined things between them. She could see now that he had been immediately skeptical about that second plea. He hadn't understood how important it was to her to try to resolve her father's anger. It wasn't surprising, she supposed, given that he was a man who'd had almost no family, and had lost even that years before.

She'd made that second request for more time; he hadn't understood why, and his lack of understanding had triggered the first questions and doubts in his mind...and he'd gone to her father, offering to buy her. But why money? she asked herself. Had John heard business rumors that her father had suffered some losses and was hard up for cash? Or was John such a cynic that he thought each person had a price?

Either way, the result had been the same. John had offered money; her father had quickly accepted; John had paid, then cultivated his dark suspicions. A set-up job, a scam, he'd decided, believing that she and her father had been working together...and now John's mind was closed. He'd never believe she was innocent!

But did that matter? she brooded. Did she want to be married to a man who had bought her—bought his way into her family and its social status? Did he love her at all? Had he ever loved her, ever seen her as more than a quick way to advance himself? Would things ever change——?

Stop! she told herself. These were all questions she'd asked herself too many times; to ask them again was an exercise in futility. There might never be clear answers, she knew, curling up in John's bed, depression settling over her like a pall.

She hadn't expected to sleep and was surprised to wake up to find the light fading, the bedroom a twilight world of vague shadows. Listlessly, she gathered up the clothes scattered on the floor, leaving hers on the bed before carrying John's into his dressing room. There she lingered, inspecting his suits in the antique armoire, the rack of ties in the small cupboard, the drawers of precisely folded shirts, the monogrammed brushes and the one pair of gold cuff links on the plain dresser.

She was trapped, she thought, fingering one of the cuff links. She had no choice; she had to live here, with this man. She had to endure this farce of a marriage, one without love, without understanding...which was what she supposed she'd been looking for here. She'd hoped to learn something about John and the way his mind worked, but there was nothing here. His personal possessions were starkly impersonal; their neat organization provided no clues to the man. All they told her was that John traveled alone, leaving no tracks.

Which you already knew, she thought, going into the bathroom for a long and leisurely soak in the bath. By the time she climbed out to dry herself her skin was flushed to a soft rosy pink; her hair, carelessly tied back with a narrow ribbon, was damp and willfully curling. This wasn't the way she wanted John to see her, she realized, reaching for her robe, determined to hurry. By the time he got home she would be dressed—and cool and poised, she promised herself, starting back to the bedroom.

But John was already home, and very much at his ease, leaning back in the bentwood rocker, his long legs stretched out, crossed at the ankle. Except for having loosened his discreetly striped tie, he was still the proper Bostonian in his well-tailored suit and crisp white linen, a cool, self-possessed and elegant figure.

"I wasn't sure you'd be here," he began, favoring her with a brief, unreadable smile. "I'm surprised that you haven't already cleared your things out of here. Now that Cynthia's gone—you do know that she's left us, don't you?—I thought you might go back to your chaste little cell."

"I——" She stopped, biting her lip. She should have moved back down to the guest room, but the thought hadn't even entered her mind... and not just because of Lillian's visit, Serena acknowledged. She'd been behaving strangely even before—what could be stranger than the fact that she hadn't even considered going to work? She'd been drifting all day, ignoring the realities of her position... It made no sense at all, and it certainly wasn't something she could explain to John! "I..." she began again, trying to think of any excuse. "I haven't had time," she offered inadequately.

"You've had all day," he pointed out, watching her closely. "Surely time enough if that was what you wanted to do? So perhaps..." Suddenly he was on his feet, smiling as he came toward her. "What was it, Serena? Did you decide that you'd like to stay, after all?"

"No!" She watched him warily, backing away from his dark and powerful figure until she found herself caught up against one of the bedposts. "You ought to know better than that."

"But I don't—not after last night." He stopped just before her, still smiling. "Don't be coy with me now, sweetheart—not after last night," he murmured, his eyes glittering dangerously. "Whether you want to admit it or not, last night was something special."

"Last night was an aberration, not like me..." She trailed off awkwardly, tucking her hands behind her to nervously finger the bedpost, wondering how to explain—what to explain! "I—I'd been drinking saki."

"Not very much—I kept track," he explained, laughing when he saw her outraged expression.

"Checking on me?" she demanded. "Afraid that I would get drunk?"

"Making sure that you didn't so you wouldn't have an excuse...if the evening ended the way that I wanted it to."

"You had it planned," she accused, standing her ground—not that she had much choice, given the bedpost against her back. "You were that sure!"

"No. I'm never sure about you," he told her, an abstracted light in his eyes, "and all I could do was hope...I still do." He took a step forward. "Serena...sweetheart, don't make things any harder than they've already been. This marriage can be more than a farce, and last night is something to build on..." He touched the ribbon holding back her wild curls, then gently teased it away. "Why not admit it? You invited what happened last night...and enjoyed it as much as I did."

"Yes, you'd like to believe that," she countered, fighting the sudden constriction in her throat. She knew what he was doing...could feel the powerful current already running between them... Not again! she vowed, marshaling her resolve. "You want to be able to have your fun and not feel guilty about it!"

"Not true," he corrected absently, playing with her curls, feathering them with his fingers. "This is for both of us."

"I don't want it," she cried, gripping the bedpost as though her life depended on it. "John, let me go!"

"Never." He shook his head, watching her face with complete absorption, like a man in a trance. "Not now... not ever, sweetheart."

"But we can't live this way," she objected weakly, trying to control her racing heartbeat, to resist the warm lassitude already invading her bones. "We'll never be happy."

"We were last night," he murmured, his lips tasting hers briefly. "Remember?"

"No, I told you——" She caught her breath when he kissed her again, knowing he'd won when her hands loosened their grip on the bedpost. "You don't play fair," she complained, going willingly when he drew her into his arms.

"It's better like this," he told her, smiling when her hands crept up to rest on his shoulders. "You'll see... we'll make something of this arrangement, forget how it started..."

Forget? No, she'd never forget, she thought sadly, but that didn't change how she felt when he kissed her like this—parting her lips, coaxing her to respond. Now her hands were gripping his shoulders with the same force as they'd once gripped the bedpost, holding on for dear life—which was true, she acknowledged. She needed this much, at least—the illusion of closeness, the pretense of love...

She tried to ignore the alien sound, resenting the intrusion, resenting John even more when he broke off their kiss. "Saved by the bell," he teased, laughing, "but not for long."

He moved away, and she sank down on the edge of the bed, afraid that her legs wouldn't hold her, not bothering to listen when he answered the phone, spoke briefly, and then turned back to her.

"You're safe for a while," he advised, his poise intact, she noted unhappily. "That was Lillian—there's a command performance tonight, a little family party to celebrate Gregory's arrival on the scene. Apparently he and Cynthia have patched things up."

The evening began as one of Lillian's little dinner parties—perfectly executed in spite of the fact that she'd had only a few hours' notice. Dinner was strictly family: Josiah Stuart and his wife Mabel, Cynthia and Gregory, Serena and John, her father and Lillian, plus Gregory's much older sister and her middle-aged husband. It was about the least interesting group Lillian had ever had at her table, in Serena's opinion—inevitable, she supposed, given the people included.

She was stuck between Gregory and his brother-in-law, neither of whom had much to say. The brother-in-law was just plain dull, while Gregory—who usually had an easy, casual charm—appeared to have been struck dumb. He spent most of the meal eyeing Cynthia and his father with wary respect—and no wonder, Serena thought. A few days before, Cynthia had walked out on him, and he'd probably thought that their marriage was over; now he'd been peremptorily summoned back to Boston to learn that everything had been patched up—without any effort on his part.

Serena actually felt a little sorry for him, although his silence created a vacuum which Mabel Stuart gladly filled. She leaned forward, ignoring her son-in-law, to subject Serena to a stern lecture on the importance of taking her "proper" place in society. "My dear, it's all very well to get an education," Mrs. Stuart began, "but don't you think you're carrying it a bit too far?"

"I hadn't thought so," Serena responded, gritting her teeth. "Do you?"

"Well, you wouldn't want to make a career of it, would you?" Mrs. Stuart countered. "Not when there's so much you could be doing—charity work and the social niceties that mean so much. Socially, your husband can use all the help he can get, and of course you were born to assume a certain position. You could be a social leader some day if you begin now and choose wisely—supporting the ballet, perhaps, and on the committee to raise funds to cure one of the better diseases..."

Mrs. Stuart had a lot more to say, but Serena tuned out, ignoring the plans for her social future. Across the table, John was seated between Cynthia and Gregory's sister but being monopolized by Gregory's father—"A chance to get to know you, my boy," Mr. Stuart had said with hearty condescension, which was about as close to being pleasant as he ever got, Serena reflected. She'd never liked him; he was too full of his own importance, and he played the proper Bostonian to the hilt. He had just the right brahmin accent and the right old-school tie; he sat on the right boards, supported the right charities. How can John stand him? she wondered, then realized what a silly question that was. This dinner-table conversation with Josiah Stuart was John's payoff for services rendered and might lead to all kinds of desirable contacts. Under the circumstances, John would stand the prosy old bore very well and was probably relishing every dull word.

After dinner, by prearrangement, a number of Cynthia's and Gregory's friends arrived; "Some fun for the young people," Lillian explained, urging them into the back drawing room where there would be dancing to the sophisticated sound system. Serena's father, John and Mr. Stuart retreated to the library; Lillian directed Mrs. Stuart and her daughter to the morning room, a quick gesture keeping Serena from following them.

"No, wait just a moment," Lillian murmured discreetly. "Your father wants a chance to speak to you this evening, and I just wanted to warn you...he doesn't know what we talked about this morning, has no idea——"

"That I know about my mother and all," Serena finished for her, the two of them briefly awkward. "Don't worry, Lil. I won't tell him."

"It would break his heart if he knew that you knew. He never wanted you to," Lillian said, clearly distressed. "I shouldn't have told you—wouldn't have if I hadn't thought..."

"No, it's all right," Serena assured her. "It's better, I think, that I do know, but I'd never hurt him. Look, you go on, you've got to entertain——"

"I know—those two crashing bores." Lillian made a face. "You don't need to join us. I expect the dancing won't be as dull, and Gregory's father shouldn't keep John that much longer. You go have some fun," she finished, producing a gracious smile as she disappeared into the morning room.

In no mood to join the dancing, Serena was briefly alone in the large central hall. Obeying a sudden impulse, she moved to the ornately carved staircase and slowly climbed the broad steps, leaving behind the sounds of music and laughter...just like old times, she thought—a party going on, and I'd rather be left alone. Upstairs, she went straight to her old room, glad to have some time to herself. This was a chance to take stock, she decided; so much of her childhood seemed somehow changed now that she knew the truth about her mother.

She switched on a light and saw that the room was just as she had left it on her wedding day. Nothing changed here; only she was different. She even looked different, she realized when she paused to examine herself in the full-length mirror on the far wall. To show off her topaz drop earrings she'd worn her hair up in her usual twist, and her dress was to her usual taste—simple lines and conservative in style and color. It was a white wool crêpe, sleeveless, with a high neckline, the long skirt swirling around her ankles, revealing a glimpse of her white strappy evening sandals with their stiletto heels. Nothing so very different from what she'd worn many times in the past, but the effect tonight was somehow more dramatic. She looked...less inhibited, perhaps, less restrained...more alive? she wondered, then turned away from the mirror when she heard a knock at the door.

"Yes? Who is it?" she called.

"All right to come in?" her father asked, opening the door just a crack. "No one seemed to know where you were," he explained when she'd told him to come in, "but I guessed you'd be up here." He smiled, a distinguished figure in his evening clothes, but looking tired and worn, Serena thought with a pang. "You never were a great one for parties."

She shrugged, returning his smile. "The Stuarts aren't really my favorite people."

"Nor mine," he allowed with a grimace, "although Gregory was a good match for Cynthia, and now that they've patched things up her future's assured. Did you know that Josiah is going to bring Gregory back to Boston? By Christmas, he says, which means that Cynthia will only have to spend two more months there. She hated it so..." He broke off, shaking his head, turning to study a collection of photographs on the wall. "But what about you, chick?" he continued after a pause. "Lil said she went to see you this morning, that you told her John is holding against you the—ah, the terms of our agreement." He turned back to her, clearly distressed. "Is that true?"

"To a certain extent," Serena answered. There was no point in trying to lie if Lillian had already told him, but Serena didn't want him worrying—not when he'd done so much for her! "But it's not a real problem,

Dad," she assured him. "I think it left an unpleasant impression, but nothing he won't get over, given time."

"But surely he knows that it wasn't your idea?" Ted Wright protested. "If he's got it into his head that you were involved I can tell him, explain."

"I don't think that would help," Serena said carefully, perching on the side of the bed, running her fingers over the bedspread's intricate design, "not just now. He wouldn't want to believe you."

"But he'd have to," her father blustered. "Why shouldn't he?"

"Because he's headstrong and proud, and the whole idea takes a little getting used to. But," she continued, using the same argument her father had used on her wedding day, "it's not as though we don't love each other!" She swallowed the painful lump in her throat, finding it almost too hard to lie about what she desperately wished could be true. "How we felt about each other last summer—that hasn't changed."

"Well…if you're sure?" he asked, doubt warring with relief and the hope that he was going to avoid a difficult scene. "I don't want you to be unhappy."

"I'm not," Serena assured him, forcing a smile. "Don't most newlywed couples go through a period of adjustment? This is just ours, so don't worry, Dad. Things will be fine!"

"Good. I'm glad to hear that," he said heartily. "Lil had me concerned, but if you're sure…"

"Oh, very sure, although there is one thing," she added casually. "John seems to think that you told him—that is, that you said I knew about the agreement. I don't quite understand that."

"But you did," her father said, looking surprised. "He came to me privately at the reception, told me that, while it went without saying, he wanted to be sure that I'd never tell you about it. Of course, by that time Cynthia had already let it slip and we'd talked about it. I had to tell him! I couldn't lie, but we didn't have a great deal of time... Perhaps I didn't explain myself clearly enough. He might have thought I was saying that you'd known about it all along.''

"I think that's what did happen, but I'll explain," Serena said with false brightness, imagining the impossibility of getting John to believe any of this. "I suspect that's the whole problem—a simple misunderstanding. Don't worry, Dad.''

"I won't, as long as my girl is happy," he told her, dropping a kiss on her cheek. "I just wanted to be sure. He's a good man, Serena. He'll take good care of you." He smiled, looking years younger. "Both my girls, settled and happy. That's what I've always wanted.''

"And that's what you've got," Serena said firmly, ignoring any number of grim realities—hers and Cynthia's—that her father didn't need to know existed. "Now, you've been up here quite a while. Don't you think Lil could use some moral support?"

"With the Stuarts? Yes," her father said, laughing, giving Serena another kiss before he left the room.

Alone again, Serena sat motionless on the bed, thinking. It hadn't been easy to string together the series of lies; it would have been even harder if her father hadn't wanted to be convinced. Tonight she'd seen what she'd missed before—that he'd aged badly in this past year. It seemed likely that his business problems had all but destroyed his confidence and his peace of mind. Given all that he'd done for her, marrying John was, she supposed, a small price for her to pay. She would think of it that way from now on—remember what her father, and Lillian of course, had done to protect her.

CHAPTER TEN

SERENA had been six when her mother died; there was only a vague recollection of the intense dark-haired woman who came and went at odd hours and rarely spent time with Serena, preferring to leave her to the care of a plump, jolly nanny in the nursery suite at the top of the house. Serena hadn't received much mothering in those early years; the loving constant in her life had been her father. Funny, she reflected, how she kept calling him that, how she would never stop thinking of him as her father. She couldn't do anything else because he'd always been there for her—especially during her first six years when she would otherwise have been terribly lonely. She knew now, thanks to Lillian's morning visit, that her father had been living a double life during those years, yet Serena remembered him as always having had plenty of time for her—reading stories to her, playing games, taking her for outings in the public gardens.

He'd married Lillian a scrupulous year after his first wife's death, which was when everything had changed—for the better, in Serena's opinion. The house had suddenly seemed lighter and brighter and more alive. There had been laughter and parties, the four of them eating together, Cynthia's and Serena's small friends coming to play. True, she and Cynthia hadn't had much in common, Serena reflected. Young as they had been, their personalities were already very different, and Cynthia had been two years younger—still almost a baby, Serena had thought at the time. She'd already finished the first grade, while Cynthia hadn't even started kindergarten ... two years had been a big gap back then.

Two years, Serena thought; Cynthia had been two years younger, and for the first time Serena began to grasp the implications of their relative ages. Cynthia had been two years younger, born two years after Serena, yet Lillian had said... Exactly what had Lillian said? Serena forced herself to concentrate. Only this morning, Lillian had told Serena how her father knew he wasn't really her father, not in the blood sense of the word. "Long enough before you were born... he was being faithful to me," Lillian had said.

Which meant... Serena was stunned by the colossal irony of what she'd just worked out for herself. She wasn't her father's daughter, but Cynthia was—Cynthia whose "official" life story was that she was Lillian's daughter by a previous marriage, a Wright only by adoption! Cynthia was the true Wright daughter, Serena the fraud... Unbelievable! John had married her because she was a Wright, and Gregory's father had not wanted Gregory to marry Cynthia because—as Serena had heard him say during a loud and acrimonious exchange with her father—"She's not really one of the family! Who knows what her father's people were like?"

Incredible, Serena thought, and so unfair...

"Renie?" Cynthia opened the door and looked in. "What are you doing up here?"

"I——" It was like seeing a ghost, Serena thought with a shiver, then offered inadequately, "Just thinking."

"Hiding, more likely." She came into the room, face flushed and hair tumbling wildly, kicked off her shoes and sat down at Serena's dressing table. "I needed a break, and saw the light under the door," she explained, her back to the room while she inspected herself in the mirror. "You ought to come down. It's not like the old days, when you used to come up here because you didn't know enough people to want to stay. You've got John now, even if he is still stuck in the library with Gregory's father, but he won't be there all night."

"It doesn't matter," Serena said with a shrug. "I know it's important to him to spend time with Mr. Stuart."

"Mmm. A fantastic chance, really," Cynthia agreed absently, hunting through the drawers of Serena's dressing table until she came up with a comb left behind, "even if the old man's a dead bore. Still," she continued, combing her hair, "did you hear what he's doing for us? Letting us come back to Boston."

"Dad said by Christmas."

"Two months," Cynthia said dreamily. "Just two more months in that swamp, and I can thumb my nose at everyone and come home...and tonight's been so much fun. You know——" she put down the comb and turned to face Serena "—it was never Gregory I minded so much. It was being stuck there, where no one really knew who we were, and we didn't know anyone very well."

"Then you're happy?" Serena asked doubtfully.

"Happy enough," Cynthia allowed, "and I'll be happier when we're back here and settled. Mr. S is going to give us more to live on, make sure that we have a nice house. Who knows? We might even be neighbors, although we'd need something bigger...a place where we could entertain."

"But is that all?" Serena persisted as Cynthia turned back to the mirror. "Is it just things—coming back here, having more money and a house?"

"Well, that's a lot of it," Cynthia answered deliberately. "That's one of the ways we're different, you and I. I know you don't care, but those things matter to me. They're important—which is a laugh, when you think about it, because you married John. You can have whatever you want just as soon as you please, while I've got to go slow and always keep on the good side of Gregory's father."

And it could have been—should have been!—the other way around, Serena thought, watching as Cynthia worked on her hair. "Does that bother you?" she asked carefully. "Would you rather have married John?"

"Oh, forget about that," Cynthia said with a laugh. "I know I said some wild things, but that was just because I was unhappy... sick to death of living in Houston."

"But really—do you ever wish that you could have married John, or someone like John?"

"You mean someone gorgeous and wildly exciting, but with no social clout? No, to be honest. I wouldn't mind having an affair with someone like that——" she giggled "—but to be married? No, thank you. I like being Mrs. Gregory Stuart—right at the top, socially, with no questions asked. You and John are going to be fighting the battle all your lives—'Bourque? What kind of a name is that? Who were his people?'" she mimicked, laughing. "That's the great thing about marrying up when you're a woman. People begin to forget who you were, because you aren't that any more. Look at Mummy. Most people have forgotten that she was no one when she and Daddy got married."

"But part of that is because she never makes a mistake," Serena pointed out. "She does things so well."

"She had to learn to do things so well," Cynthia countered dispassionately, "and I already know. It won't take me as long to be completely accepted."

"And yet... it still doesn't seem fair."

"Oh, nothing's really fair in life," Cynthia shrugged. "I've never let that bother me."

"But——" Serena drew a deep breath, unable to let the issue drop now "—do you remember what you said when we had lunch with John?"

"Yesterday," Cynthia supplied with an unreadable smile. "Seems like a year, doesn't it?"

"But do you remember?"

"Renie, I said a lot of things. Who knows which ones I remember and which ones I don't?"

"About the real family scandal."

Cynthia shrugged. "I told you. I made that up."

"Honestly?" Serena asked carefully. "I don't think you did."

"Well you should," Cynthia said emphatically—not angry, just very sure of herself. "Family scandals are water over the dam. They ought to be left alone."

"But..." Serena paused, then, sure that Cynthia knew, she said frankly, "this one's so unfair."

"I don't think so!" Cynthia set down the comb with a decided snap. "Let's assume—just for the moment— that we both know what we're talking about, and that it's true. You think it's unfair, and I don't. I think it's one of life's compromises—the best possible kind! Do you realize that there's never been a breath of scandal about Mummy—or me? As far as the world knows, Mummy is someone Dad met after your mother died. Everyone knows that Mummy was a young widow, trying to raise a child on her own. She might have been a social nobody, but there's no harm—and no scandal!—in that. Serena..." Cynthia turned to face her, her light blue eyes intent "...I may not be a Wright, except by adoption, but that doesn't matter. I don't need that protection, but you do! Do you see?"

"How did you find out?" Serena asked, her voice barely above a whisper. "When did you know?"

"I don't know—not for sure—but a few people have talked. I suppose..." Cynthia shrugged "...maybe they knew your mother, or knew something about her. I've always laughed, asked if anyone knows anyone who's more of a straitlaced Puritan than you are. That usually does the trick. Don't worry, Renie! It doesn't matter!"

"But——" Funny, Serena reflected. She'd said the same thing to her father not long before, but it was easier to give reassurance than to accept it. "It still doesn't seem fair."

"It does to me! It would to you, too, if you weren't such a straitlaced Puritan! Look, Renie, Dad did his best to protect all three of us, and I think he did a very good job. I also happen to think that Mummy and I got the best of the bargain...and if you ever—ever!—bring this up again and go bleating on about how it isn't fair I shall slap you. So there! Besides," she added with a guileless smile, "we don't know—either one of us—if it's true."

"I do! I'm sure——"

"Sure?" Cynthia seized on the word. "You can't be sure—not absolutely! You weren't there, were you? You can't know—no one can! And come on," she commanded, getting up, grabbing Serena's hand and giving a tug, "I've had enough of this kind of talk. I want to go back to the party, and you're coming too."

"I don't want—I don't think..." Serena protested feebly.

"Well I do! Come on, Renie, have some fun—at least make the best of it," she qualified when she saw Serena's expression. "I'm not taking no for an answer!"

Downstairs, there was still no sign of John. "Well, he's certainly a success with Gregory's father," Cynthia observed, "but if he doesn't appear in ten minutes I'm going to go into that library and make him come out!" In the meantime she found someone to dance with Serena, who excused herself as soon as she decently could. She retreated to the edge of the room, near the door, her mind busy with what Cynthia had said to her in the bedroom.

How could she not mind? Serena wondered. How could she stand all the pretense, the polite fiction that cloaked the whole sorry mess. How could——?

"Dance with me." John materialized beside her and broke into her reverie, and she stared up at him with blank, uncomprehending eyes. "Dance with me," he said again.

It was an order, she noted, not a request; he gave her no choice. Just my luck! she thought grimly as he led her on to the makeshift dance floor. It was bad enough to be forced to abandon the thoughts which had just turned her world upside-down, and even worse that someone had just selected something slower and more romantic for the sound system, and someone else had dimmed the lights. Serena drew a deep breath, steeling herself to endure the kind of physical contact she desperately wished to avoid.

"Relax, sweetheart," John advised as he drew her into his arms, his damnably knowing smile making it clear that she'd given herself away. "Will this really be such an ordeal?"

Worse than that! she thought, refusing to answer, nervously biting her lip as she struggled to avoid missing a step. They had never danced together before; she wasn't prepared for its devastating effect on her. It wasn't easy to be this close to him—to feel his breath stirring her hair, to inhale the heady mix of his masculine scent and crisp after-shave.

"Nothing to say?" he asked after a moment.

"I'm concentrating...trying not to trip over your feet."

"Am I such a bad dancer?"

"No," she answered crossly. He knew perfectly well that he wasn't; in fact, he was very good, which was part of her problem. "But I am."

"Not with someone else," he objected smoothly. "I saw you."

"I don't see how! You've spent the whole evening in the library with Gregory's father."

"Not the whole evening, sweetheart, and you looked to be enjoying yourself when I saw you."

"I was making the best of things—Cynthia's advice."

"Ah, Cynthia...a wise girl."

"Yes," Serena agreed, experiencing a quick pang of guilt. "You should have married her."

"She was already taken," he pointed out, amused. "Besides, I didn't want her. I wanted you."

Wanted, she thought; wanted, not loved... "What you wanted was a wife with the very best family background."

"So you keep telling me," he agreed carelessly, "and it must be true. I'm here tonight, thanks to you, permitted to mingle with the very best of the Boston brahmins, although..." he paused consideringly, using the moment to draw Serena closer "...I've been permitted to do more than just mingle with Josiah Stuart, haven't I? I've had several hours of his nearly undivided attention."

"A signal honor," Serena agreed sarcastically. "You must be pleased."

"More struck by the hypocrisy of the whole business. I kept the lid on his son's marriage, so he owes me one. You've got to admit, it's cold-blooded."

"Of course," Serena agreed, but without really thinking. Suddenly she was caught up in the hitherto unknown—but definitely heady—attraction of following his body's lead...which was what dancing was all about, she realized in a blinding flash of insight. Until now she'd never known—couldn't possibly have imagined—that dancing was about the awareness of another's physical presence, about being attuned to the one you loved, about responding, following where he led... just like last night, when—— No! She would not think of last night, she decided, pushing the memories back. "It might have been cold-blooded," she said, picking up the thread of the conversation—better, by far, to stick to the present!—"but maybe...at least I hope Cynthia and Gregory can be happy."

"Happy?" John repeated skeptically. "From what I've seen of this crowd, happiness doesn't count. Expediency's the thing. Cynthia, given a little time for sober reflection, decided that she didn't want to lose the advantage of being Mrs. Gregory Stuart. Gregory probably didn't care what happened, so long as he avoided the scandal of a divorce in the family. It's the way you people operate. Look at what you did!'' He paused—for dramatic effect, she wondered, or to give her an instant to brace herself for the unpleasantness to follow? ''You made the supreme sacrifice—saved Daddy's reputation and made the family solvent again—by marrying beneath your station.''

''That isn't true,'' she said fiercely. ''I never thought of it—of you!—that way. Never! How can you—didn't you get to know me well enough to realize that I'd never think of you that way?''

''What's this?'' he asked, confusing her with his smile. ''Last summer's game?''

''I——'' She stopped, staring up at him with anguished eyes. Last summer's game; not last summer's girl. Last summer's girl meant nothing to him; he'd just made that clear, and in the same instant Serena had discovered that she desperately wanted to be last summer's girl. She'd give anything she possessed to be back there again—in the summer, when it had seemed that they were in love.

''What's the matter, sweetheart?'' he persisted when she remained silent, taunting her with his smile. ''Cat got your tongue?''

''No.'' Her steps faltered; it was hard to keep dancing when she'd just caught a glimpse of the rest of her life... No, she'd caught more than a glimpse; she could see the rest of her life with blinding clarity: a lifetime of John's disbelief and verbal torment, a lifetime without love— it was more than she could bear. Suddenly she couldn't breathe; she was going to faint—faint or do something she would never be able to take back. She had to get out, get away. ''Go to hell, John,'' she whispered fiercely, freeing herself from his embrace.

Head bent, she pushed through the other dancers, no idea where she was going except away from John. She had to get out, find a place where she'd be able to breathe—if John would let her escape. She could actually feel him following her, gaining on her as she left the back drawing room.

"Lovers' quarrel, my boy?" she heard Mr. Stuart inquire, his hearty voice booming out over the music. "Both those girls need taming. You and Gregory will have your hands full if you don't..."

Mr. Stuart speaking to John, Serena realized, realizing, too, how ironic that was. Mr. Stuart was the one man John couldn't afford to ignore; being polite would tie up for at least a couple of minutes—long enough for her to make her escape.

"Serena?" In the central hall Lillian materialized before her, a puzzled frown marring her brow. "Darling, where are you going?"

"Out," she answered shortly, in a fever to be gone, "for some fresh air."

"But it's too late to go out alone. I'll get John."

"Don't bother—he's talking to Mr. Stuart." Serena had reached the door, had it open. "I won't be long," she lied as she closed it behind her.

She gathered up her skirt and ran lightly down the steps, wavering briefly as she decided which way to head. The house stood at the corner of Commonwealth Avenue and Dartmouth Street; to stay on Commonwealth would be too obvious, she decided, so she cut around the corner to Marlborough, then set off toward the public gardens.

This was better, she thought, drawing a deep breath. It had turned surprisingly warm for the end of October, with a night of balmy breezes and only occasional wisps of cloud to obscure the crescent moon sailing high in the sky. A good night to be out, she decided, listening to the sound of her footsteps echoing in the quiet street. It must be late for the city to be so still—no other people in sight, almost no traffic, no lights in the houses she passed. Too late to be out alone? Not for me! she assured herself with a defiant toss of her head. Just let a mugger try to attack; she'd tear him apart!

Moving as fast as her frivolous sandals would permit, she hurried down Marlborough, crossing Clarendon, then Berkeley, without bothering to check for traffic. She was forced to stop briefly at Arlington—a couple of cruising cabs—before sprinting across toward the shadowy darkness of the public gardens. She'd made it! John couldn't find her now, she told herself as she started down one of the narrower paths, then, from behind, someone caught her arm in an iron grip.

"Of all the fool things!" Before she could panic she knew who it was—John, sounding slightly out of breath and very angry, his voice harsh in the darkness. "What the hell are you trying to do—get yourself killed?"

"What business is it of yours?"

"It damn well is my business! You're my wife!"

"I'm not your wife! I'm your possession," she accused, forced to stand motionless in his grasp, her back to him. "You're just trying to protect your investment!"

"You think so?"

"I know so! You paid for me—you throw that in my face every time," she raged. "I'm sick to death of your accusations, of being tormented and never believed, of being blamed for something I didn't do! If I hear one more word about how much you paid for me, I'll—I'll——"

"You'll what?" he inquired, dangerous quiet replacing his anger. "What will you do?"

"I don't know! Scream, or hit you," she threatened wildly.

"Why not leave me?" he invited, finally forcing her to turn and face him, only then relaxing his grip on her arm. "If you're as innocent as you'd like me to believe why let things continue? You can walk out——"

"You know I can't do that." The satisfying release of anger was gone in a flash, destroyed by cold reality. "My father..."

"Why so noble?" John persisted. "Why protect him when it's making you so unhappy? I told you—he won't go to jail. Surely he'd be willing to suffer a little embarrassment——?"

"I can't do that—couldn't ask him——"

"Of course not," he agreed with an unpleasant smile. "Maintaining appearances—that's all that matters to people like you. You'll do anything to keep his dirty little secret for him—he'll make you do whatever it takes!"

"You would think that, but you're wrong!" She glared at him, her anger back with a vengeance, pushing her beyond the limits of prudence or discretion. "You're cold all the way through! You don't know what it means to love someone, to care what happens to anyone but yourself. You'd never go out of your way to protect anyone else, but my father has been protecting me all my life... I'm not his. I'm—I don't really know who I am," she said unsteadily, the facts of her existence finally real for her in the telling. She was possessed by a wealth of emotion which threatened to overwhelm her, no longer even aware that she was telling her story to John. "My mother was—was a tramp. She slept around...but not with—with... He knew he wasn't my father," Serena continued, on the edge of incoherence. "Nobody knows who my father was but he made sure that no one found out. He's let me think—let everyone think—that I'm his daughter, but I'm not... He's been protecting me all my life, and if I protect him now—well, it's the least I can do...the only way to repay him for all those years."

"Serena—why didn't you tell me?"

"I didn't know." Nor had she known she was crying until John handed her his handkerchief...John. She'd forgotten that John was here; now that she knew she realized that there was even more to this whole sorry business. "That's another thing you're not going to believe," she said, wiping her eyes. "I only found out this morning."

"How convenient," he murmured—just as she'd known he would.

"It wasn't meant to be convenient," she snapped, now too angry for tears, his handkerchief crumpled in her clenched fist. "Lillian told me, but only because I said I was going to divorce you, that I didn't care what it did to my father. I told her I didn't see why I should when he'd cared more about money than about me. That's why she told me, because what I intended to do would have wounded him terribly. She wasn't thinking about his reputation, or about maintaining appearances! She was thinking about all the years he'd protected me——"

"All the years he'd maintained appearances," John put in smoothly, but Serena was having none of that.

"No! It wasn't about maintaining appearances—not when I was a baby... a child! I was six when my mother died—not that she'd ever been much of a mother. I hardly remember her, but I do remember my father, the things he did with me... And when she died——" Serena was crying again, dabbing ineffectually at her eyes with John's handkerchief "—I would have been all alone if he hadn't been there. I was a bastard—I still am, but——"

"Don't talk nonsense," John said harshly, seizing her by the shoulders. "I don't want to hear——"

"Why not?" she demanded through her tears, waiting for him to shake her. "It's true! I realize you didn't get what you paid for—I mean, I'm not really my father's daughter. You paid to be connected to the Wrights, and you're not—not really! You'll have to decide if the appearance is enough, or——"

"For goodness' sake," he snapped, his fingers biting into her flesh. "Stop it, Serena!"

"—or if——" remarkably he didn't shake her; instead she felt herself being drawn toward him "—or if you want a divorce," she finished, folding into his arms, her words muffled against the starched white of his shirt.

"I don't want a divorce."

"But some people know," she wailed. "At least, they suspect."

"I don't want a divorce," he said again. "It's all right, Serena—be quiet."

"But Cynthia told me——"

"I don't care about that." He stopped, creating just enough distance between them to permit him to see her face. "I don't want a divorce," he said for the third time. "I want you. I always have."

"But——"

"Serena, be quiet!" Now he did shake her, but very gently. "I wanted you from that first day, when you were obviously as attracted to me as I was to you—until we got to the graveyard and you found those stones carved by——"

"JN," she supplied, fixing on the one thing in what he was saying that she could comprehend.

"At which point you forgot all about me...and I stopped just wanting you—and fell in love."

"Why?" she asked with the breath she'd been holding.

"I don't know why," he confessed with a heart-stopping smile. "Because you were so artless—so happy, so absorbed by your discovery. There was this luminous innocence about you, and I knew I wasn't going to get over you."

"But once we were married, you said——"

"Yes, I know what I said," he agreed, his expression pained, "but by that time I was convinced that you were lying through your teeth. So many things had gone wrong, Serena, starting on the night of the Fourth, when I took you home and your father was so angry. It didn't make sense, at the time—although, now that you've told me about your mother, I can see what must have been in his mind—why he overreacted and kept on overreacting...

"You were right about one thing—I did offer him money," John admitted steadily, holding her gaze with the intensity of his own, "not to buy you or buy my way into your family, but to find some way to break the impasse. I went to him, asked him what I could do, what it would take to make him change his mind. I'd heard that he'd suffered some pretty big losses, and money was the one thing I knew I had to offer. I named a sum and said it was his, to cover his losses, so long as I could be sure that he'd done nothing illegal. In exchange, all I asked was that he gave his permission, whatever it took to stop making you so desperately unhappy.

"Even then I didn't doubt you," John continued after a moment. "It wasn't until just after the wedding when I found a moment to speak to him. I told him we both had to be careful, that you must never find out what we'd done. I'll never forget how he stood there, stared at me and then said that you knew everything. It poleaxed me. I'd been so sure you were different—as innocent and as sweet as you appeared to be...but that blew up in my face. If you knew—and your father said that you did—then you were a party to an incredibly bizarre arrangement. This was extortion masquerading as marriage! On the spot I decided that I'd made all the wrong assumptions, been a fool—the one time in my life I hadn't been a skeptic about what life seemed to be offering."

"But you said——" Serena paused, biting her lip. "After the wedding, when I tried to explain, you said that you'd only married me to become an insider. You said—I'll never forget this—that proper Boston would never close its doors to you again."

"I was angry, Serena," he said, his expression twisted, pain lurking in his eyes. "I'd been hurt, my pride had taken a hell of a beating. I know now that I had it all wrong, but at the time it all seemed to make perfect sense—why else would you have married me, given my manifest inadequacies——?''

"Inadequacies?" she asked, peering up at him through her tears. "What inadequacies?"

"No breeding, no background, no education, all my rough edges...."

"But I never cared about those things," she protested. "They didn't matter!"

"They did to me," he countered grimly, "which is why it was so easy for me to believe that love had nothing to do with why you were marrying me."

"And I was believing the same thing about you. John——" She stopped, biting her lip again. He'd talked about things making perfect sense, and what he'd said seemed to—if she could believe him! "You really didn't care about family connections and wanting to socialize with the best people—all that proper Boston stuff?"

"No, my love," he said with the slightest hint of a smile. "I never have. If I've been seen at some of the bigger—and least exclusive—parties it's because I'm happy to support certain charities. But care about social acceptance?" He shook his head. "That's never mattered to me. I'm successful—my buildings are accepted—because I believed in building well. It's quality that sells what I build—not the social contacts I make."

"But . . . those parties we went to with Cynthia, and tonight," she reminded him, still doubting, or still afraid to believe, "you——"

"Seemed to know what I was doing?" he suggested, amused. "Possibly even appeared to fit in?"

"Of course you did, but that doesn't take any great genius," she declared. "The only difference between you and most of those social types is that you're probably more polite—and a whole lot less boring!"

"Oh, Serena!" He laughed, then looked at her for a long moment, an abstracted light in his eyes. "That's more like last summer's girl, the one I first met. Do you know what I thought when Serena Winslow Wright wrote, asking to look at my graveyard? I thought she'd be the worst kind of snob, looking for more illustrious ancestors—either that or a dried-up old spinster. To say the least, you were not what I expected . . . particularly not that first night at dinner, when you made it clear that you thought I was too sensitive about this class business."

"You were so capable and assured," she remembered, "so impressive that it was hard to believe that you cared."

"Then let me confess. I never had been before, but I suddenly realized that I was sitting across the table from a Winslow and a Wright—the very bluest of blue bloods! I couldn't think of you as just another attractive girl—much less as the girl I'd fallen in love with in the course of one afternoon. You were worlds away from me, completely out of my league."

"What?" she demanded, laughing, as though she were back there, as free and uninhibited as she'd been that evening. "Out of your league?"

"That's what I thought," he assured her, "until you wound up and let fly about ancestors—about your *Mayflower* ancestor, dead drunk under the family tree."

John Billington," she supplied.

"Whoever. It doesn't matter who it was—it was just that you didn't care. Ancestor worship obviously wasn't your thing, and I thought—well, there's hope yet for this poor peasant boy."

"John, don't call yourself that," she said, fiercely partisan—just as she had been that first evening. "You're not——" She stopped, urgency suddenly displaced by laughter. "You're hardly a boy, and you're not poor, and if you're a peasant then save me from blue bloods!

I never wanted a blue blood, anyway, and once I'd met you... John," she asked, holding her breath, "is it really as easy as this?"

"Lord, I hope so," he said fervently, drawing her closer, "if you can believe me—and forgive me for what I did, the things I said. I don't have an excuse, except that I'd been on the outside for so long—emotionally, not socially," he qualified quickly. "I'd been careful not to let anyone get too close, hadn't wanted anyone near me—until that day in the graveyard..."

He paused to draw a deep breath. "Serena, I don't think there's any really easy way out of this mess. There don't seem to be any absolutes—neither of us can prove we're telling the truth, although I do believe you now. What I was paranoid enough to think was a carefully constructed plot—that incredible scene with your father, your reluctance to do anything until he stopped being so angry—was really no plot at all. It really was nothing more than a cosmic misunderstanding, and some past history that neither of us knew at the time."

"You do believe that?" she asked carefully.

"Yes, absolutely," he said gravely, "but the question is—can you believe that I reacted the way I did out of pride and anger and because I'm not nearly as self-confident as you seem to think I am? From the start it had been hard for me to believe that someone like you would actually want to marry someone like me——"

"I'm afraid that *is* hard to believe," she said, on the edge of nervous laughter. "John Bourque—insecure?"

"Damned insecure—when it came to you," he admitted with a self-conscious smile. "I told you—you were out of my league, lady!"

"And I thought you were out of mine—which was why it was easy for me to believe that you'd just married me for what I could do for you socially... and why I was jealous of Cynthia," she added candidly. "I was sure you had, or would—well, you know what!"

"Yes," he agreed, a smile tugging at the corners of his mouth, "which is why I got her to stay with us in the first place—hoping that you might be jealous, or that something about her visit might jar us out of the frozen pattern we'd been in since the wedding."

"It jarred me, all right," Serena allowed—her turn for a self-conscious smile, "jarred me into doing a striptease for you."

"Ah, yes," he murmured with a reminiscent smile, "that incredible, glorious striptease... That was when I finally began to believe that there might be a happy ending after all."

"Only that there *might* be?" she asked, stumbling on this one point. "How could you not believe? I was honest afterward. I told you I loved you!"

"But it seemed ... too much like the pattern of maintaining appearances, I suppose. You'd been fighting so hard—against that aspect of things in particular—and I was afraid you were trying to justify what had just happened." He paused to study her face, saw the doubt still in her eyes. "Serena, think about it—how would you have felt just then if I'd announced that I loved you? Would you have believed?"

"I don't know," she admitted uncomfortably. "I wanted to believe that you did...I might have, at that moment, until the next thing came along to make me doubt it."

"But do you believe it now?" he asked carefully. "Do you believe me when I tell you that I love you—more than life itself?"

"Yes," she answered simply, then saw the question in his eyes and added, "both—I believe you...and I love you too."

"Is that a fact?" he murmured, smiling down at her.

She nodded, watching, hypnotized, while he bent his head, her lips already parted when his mouth closed over hers. He kissed her with a fierce, compelling thoroughness, kindling her response and drawing her even deeper into the mystery where her need met his.

"This is crazy," he finally managed, his breathing nearly as uneven as her own. "Whenever this happens I have this mad compulsion..."

"To what?" she inquired with mock innocence, linking her arms around his neck, increasing the contact between them.

"To take the pins out of your hair," he told her, laughing when he saw her expression. "Do you remember the first time?" he teased, his fingers beginning to probe her hair, busy finding pins and scattering them on the ground. "It was magic, Serena...you were so close to me, and I felt as though I'd come home."

"So did I," she agreed dreamily, lifting her head, seeking his lips. "I wanted to stay there forever."

"So did I," he told her between kisses, threading his fingers through her hair when the pins were gone. "I do now...but this is neither the time or the place."

"I don't see why not," she objected.

"You wouldn't—bawdy Pilgrim," he teased, "but it's the middle of the night...and we're in the public gardens," he reminded her.

"I don't care if you don't."

"Sweetheart, we can't stay here," he pointed out reasonably. "We'll get arrested, or mugged..."

"I don't think so, and it's like last summer—when you almost made love to me on the grass," she told him with mock-innocent daring. "You would have if I hadn't been such a coward...but I'm braver now," she invited, on her toes to reach up to kiss him, "and it's a very warm night."

"Not that warm," he countered unsteadily. "Sweetheart, don't tempt me."

"That's the general idea—I want to."

"So I gathered," he agreed, briefly returning her kiss, "but I want a bed. Let's go home, love."

"There were fireworks last time," she reminded him, "and if we stay here we can look at the moon and the stars and pretend... If we go home there won't be any fireworks."

"But there will be," he promised. "Sweetheart... last summer's girl, we'll make our own."

And they did.

Let

HARLEQUIN ROMANCE®

take you

BACK TO THE

Come to the Circle Q Ranch, near Yerington, Nevada!

Meet "cattle king" Zack Quinn, a wealthy and well-connected rancher. And meet Alexandria Duncan, small-business owner and surrogate parent....

Read THE RANCHER AND THE REDHEAD by Rebecca Winters, September's Back to the Ranch title! Available in September wherever Harlequin books are sold.

RANCH4

HARLEQUIN CELEBRATES
THE SEASON OF SHARING
AND FAMILY WITH

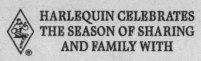

Friends, Families, Lovers

Harlequin introduces the latest member in its family of
seasonal collections. Following in the footsteps of the popular
My Valentine, Just Married and *Harlequin Historical Christmas
Stories,* we are proud to present FRIENDS, FAMILIES,
LOVERS. A collection of three new contemporary romance
stories about America at its best, about welcoming others into
the circle of love.... Stories to warm your heart ...

By three leading romance authors:

> KATHLEEN EAGLE
> SANDRA KITT
> RUTH JEAN DALE

> Available in October, wherever
> Harlequin books are sold.

THANKS

Fifty red-blooded, white-hot, true-blue hunks from every
State in the Union!

Beginning in May, look for MEN MADE IN AMERICA!
Written by some of our most popular authors, these
stories feature fifty of the strongest, sexiest men, each
from a different state in the union!

Two titles available every other month at your favorite
retail outlet.

In September, look for:

DECEPTIONS by Annette Broadrick (California)
STORMWALKER by Dallas Schulze (Colorado)

In November, look for:

STRAIGHT FROM THE HEART by Barbara Delinsky
(Connecticut)
AUTHOR'S CHOICE by Elizabeth August (Delaware)

You won't be able to resist MEN MADE IN AMERICA!

If you missed your state or would like to order any other states that have already been published, send your name, address, zip or postal code, along with a check or money order (please
do not send cash) for $3.59 for each book, plus 75¢ postage and handling ($1.00 in Canada),
payable to Harlequin Reader Service, to:

In the U.S.

3010 Walden Avenue
P.O. Box 1369
Buffalo, NY 14269-1369

In Canada

P.O. Box 609
Fort Erie, Ontario
L2A 5X3

Please specify book title(s) with order.
Canadian residents add applicable federal and provincial taxes.

MEN993

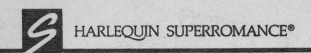

HARLEQUIN SUPERROMANCE®

HARLEQUIN SUPERROMANCE WANTS TO INTRODUCE YOU TO A DARING NEW CONCEPT IN ROMANCE...

WOMEN WHO DARE!
Bright, bold, beautiful ...
Brave and caring, strong and passionate ...
They're women who know their own minds
and will dare anything ... for love!

One title per month in 1993, written by popular Superromance authors, will highlight our special heroines as they face unusual, challenging and sometimes dangerous situations.

Dive into a whirlwind of passion and excitement next month with:
#562 WINDSTORM by Connie Bennett
Available in September wherever Harlequin Superromance novels are sold.

If you missed any of the Women Who Dare titles and would like to order them, send your name, address, zip or postal code along with a check or money order for $3.39 for #533, #537, #541, #545 and #549, or $3.50 for #553, #554 and #558, for each book ordered (do not send cash), plus 75¢ ($1.00 in Canada) for postage and handling, payable to Harlequin Reader Service, to:

In the U.S.	In Canada
3010 Walden Avenue	P.O. Box 609
P.O. Box 1325	Fort Erie, Ontario
Buffalo, NY 14269-1325	L2A 5X3

Please specify book title(s) with your order.
Canadian residents add applicable federal and provincial taxes.

WWD-S